METROPOLICKS Book 1:
A Sexy Romantic Comedy

Felicia Lin and Victor Scott Rodriguez

WWS Press
New York

WWS Press
Metropolicks Book 1: A Sexy Romantic Comedy
Felicia Lin and Victor Scott Rodriguez

Published in the United States of America by WWS Press
ISBN 978-0-9907768-3-3

Printed by Create Space, a DBA of On-Demand Publishing LLC

Metropolicks*
[mi-trop-uh-liks]

noun

1. A large, busy international city (e.g. New York City) filled with varied stories of relationship adventures and misadventures.

2. A major urban center in which sexual activity is prominent, especially those involving the use of one's tongue.

3. A fast-paced, competitive metropolis where highly ambitious people focus on licking the competition and getting ahead in dating.

* as defined on The Urban Dictionary

FOR MORE ON METROPOLICKS VISIT:
www.Metropolicks.com

ACKNOWLEDGMENTS

Writing a book is one thing, but creating a finished product is another. There are indeed many people to thank and acknowledge for making this book series happen. It is hard to know where to begin.

Thank you to Alice Heiserman, our diligent, enthusiastic content and copy editor, who added much value to the novel. We owe you a great deal.

We'd also like to acknowledge the contributions of those who gave us insights, each in their own way, into the mechanics and legalities of self-publishing: Hugh Howey, Guy Kawasaki and Shawn Welch, Maria Murnane, and Rob Thony.

Many thanks to the several romance authors who shared their experience and advice with us including: Tina DeSalvo, Debra Holland, Beverly Jenkins, Diane Kelly, Maggie Marr, Tessa McFionn, Sarah MacLean, Priscilla Oliveras, Maggie Rivers, and Cecilia Tan.

Much appreciation goes to those who offered advice and recommendations regarding the cover designs of the book series, among them are: Candace Braun Davison, Serena Chen, Joanne Louie, Johanna Salazar, and Peter Yang Zhao. We also owe thanks to Vinny Bove, Emily Chen, George Madarasz, and Michelle Shinagawa for your recommendations and expertise in making our book covers come to life. A big thank you also goes to Gilly Rosenthol, who formatted our book series. We'd also like to thank Jennie Yip and Claudine Lee who created a one-of-a-kind artwork that appears in the Metropolicks ebook.

A big debt of thanks goes to Maggie Law, our talented photographer, who tirelessly photographed several models during a marathon shoot. Among the models are: Jide Alao, Sarah Clark, Ryan Dawalt, Mieko Gavia, Jason He, Lynda Hinder, Kara Xinhang Li, Andrew Nicholas, Prakash Patil, David Rodriguez, Gabby Jiayin She, Tina Telalyan, and Pai-Sen Wang. Each one of you brought something truly unique to the shoot and your photos have been used for our promotional campaigns. But we do want to especially thank Davide Filippini and Sheila G., our Metropolicks Books 1-3 cover models. The chemistry between the two of you, as seen in your photos and the Metropolicks videos, is undeniable. Other people to thank regarding the photo shoot include: Kristin Mirabelle, our hair and makeup artist, Alice Chin, our wardrobe consultant, and the rest of the crew: Huaying Chen, Deanna Denman, Annie Lu, Sara Vinik, and Tony Wong.

We are grateful to Jami Jackson, Caesar Jackson and Blacque Records for sharing Jami's musical talent with us. Jami's songs "Let Love Live" and "Keep Walkin' On" have been featured in two Metropolicks music videos with the behind the scenes footage from the photo shoot.

And before all of this, there were our test readers. Thank you; you were the first ones to give us feedback and perspective on the novel.

We also want to specifically acknowledge the following people for their support and friendship: Juan Betancourt, David Chan, Will Chao, Nicole Chen, Donna Drake, Diana Lee, Jack Li, Supei Liu, Joanne Louie, Diana Mao, Alissa Moore, Chris Nicodemo, Krista Sande-Kerback, Nelson Searcy, Ryan Shemen, Jim Su, Kerrick Thomas, Lorie Thomas, Yue Wang, and Cindy Zhou.

And lastly, thank you to Catarina Serra and Ichi Shih for hosting a Halloween party several years ago, where we met each other for the very first time. The rest, as they say, is history.

Felicia and Victor

TABLE OF CONTENTS

BOOK 1: SPRING

BOOK 1: SUMMER

BOOK 1: FALL

BOOK 1: WINTER

INTRODUCTION

Dating in New York is not for the faint of heart. With so many singles packed into the island of Manhattan and people marrying later in life, you'd think that there would be endless opportunities to find love. However, with so many options, it is easy to find yourself going through the revolving doors of dating. There are always fresh distractions—the newer, the better, or the trendier. Who has the time or patience to make relationships work? So, are the odds really in your favor in New York if you are looking for Mr. or Ms. Right?

To have a fighting chance you'll need a plan of attack and a support system. In fact, you'll need all the help you can get. You'll need an army to win this war. This army includes your friends, those you can trust, those who you can go to with the joy and the pain of your pursuit. Don't forget your friends' friends, and your acquaintances—you never know who you'll meet through these connections. And then, you will need a backup plan. So, suit up, put on your best armor—be it a little black dress or your sharpest looking suit. Lock and load your best pickup lines or your sexiest, most charming smile, because love is a battlefield. And as the saying goes, you may have to kiss a lot of frogs before you find your prince or princess.

When you are single and have lived in New York long enough, you will probably have a few stories to share. We soon found out that this was truer than we could have imagined. As friends heard that we were working on this novel, a strange thing began happening. People started volunteering to share their dating stories with us.

While our novel was inspired in part by people's true dating experiences in New York City, these experiences were used in a fictitious manner. The novel is a work of fiction and is a result of our creative imagination. Our intention was to create characters who were composites. Therefore, any resemblance to real persons, living or dead, is purely coincidental and unintentional.

Another unusual development happened during the writing of this book—when someone gave us legal consent to be mentioned in the book by name, with the caveat that none of that individual's personal stories be included in the book. That led to several other people being mentioned in the book by their real names, and we followed the same protocol with each of them. Thus, the stories in this book are interspersed with the names of real people and real places.

In the opening scene of the book we'll introduce you to an ensemble of characters. Then, the perspective will shift into first-person narration as each character tells a tale from his or her point of view.

There are many stories to be told and others that are best kept private. We are here to tell the tales of a few New Yorkers brave enough to endure heartbreak and rejection in order to find love. In the words of the great poet Ovid, "Fortune and love favor the brave."

We wish to thank all who have contributed stories, but, of course, we can't do so by name. In order to protect people's anonymity, we have changed names, ethnicities, occupations, places of residence and identifiable physical characteristics, and in some instances, the gender, national origin, religious views, and political views of those who have volunteered stories. In every instance, we have combined several stories within the same chapter, so that every chapter is in fact composite in nature.

One last thought: when a dating relationship goes awry, don't sweat it; it is not the end of the world. How do we know it is not the end of the world? Because it is already tomorrow in Taiwan.

BOOK 1

SPRING

A Good Man is Hard to Find, but a Hard Man is a Good Find

(Tara, Frank, Montoya, Nine and Luana)

Tara Reynolds entered the gigantic rooftop bar of 230 Fifth Avenue and felt the gaze of several men as she sauntered past them in a form-fitting black dress revealing her entire back. Her long, luminous, dark hair, which reached down to the middle of her back was draped over one of her shoulders. She was in her late twenties and Asian, though one would not have guessed that from her surname.

As she scanned the room, she saw two of her male friends Frank and Montoya. Frank Branigan, a tall Irish-American, was twelve years her senior. He'd grown up in Princeton, New Jersey and was usually the most dapper man in the room. He was always impeccably dressed in custom-tailored suits. Standing beside him was Montoya, one of his closest friends. Half-Spanish and half-British, Montoya was a combination of Latin looks and British charm, thanks to his British accent. He was able to approach ladies with ease, and was the sort of person who could find something to talk about with just about anyone, which made him Frank's favorite wingman.

"Sorry I'm late," Tara apologized to Frank and Montoya, and promptly kissed each of them on the cheek. "So, good crowd?"

"Not bad," Frank said.

"Well, it looks like you are not the only one who is fashionably late," Montoya said as he pointed to the door. "Nine just arrived."

Nine Anderson was the youngest of the bunch at twenty-six years old. Lean and statuesque, with a medium-brown complexion, and dark, shoulder-length hair, her most striking feature was her green eyes. Montoya had mentored her when she was a Summer Associate at his law firm. Together, all four of them often frequented parties and mixers together, trying their luck in the endless possibilities of New York City's dating pool.

Nine hugged and kissed each of them on the cheek, "So, how are you guys doing?"

"Just chilling and checking out the crowd," Montoya replied.

Nine surveyed the crowd. They did not look like your average after-work crowd, she thought. Many of the women looked very stylish and put together, as were the men, "I have to say, it's a pretty good looking crowd," she noted.

On this beautiful spring evening, the floor-to-ceiling glass windows of the 230 Fifth Avenue penthouse lounge offered panoramic 360-degree views of the city. The sight of the Empire State Building in the near distance was even more striking from the open-air rooftop bar, which was up one flight of stairs from the penthouse lounge. With the iconic Manhattan skyline as a backdrop, it looked like a picture perfect shot of New York City's glamorous nightlife.

That night, the question on everyone's lips was, "How do you know Juan?" The Juan in question was Juan Betancourt, a top headhunter, who had started throwing parties in New York City in 2008. Today was Juan's birthday. He was of Cuban descent, had gone to Harvard, and then to Wharton where he got an MBA. On his smartphone was a contact list of more than 5,000 friends, and friends of friends. One of his claims to fame was having appeared as a guest judge on the television show, The Apprentice. Juan's parties were fast becoming a part of the New York City social scene. He was a one-man networking machine.

The penthouse lounge had on this particular night, become Juan's extended living room. Numerous seating areas consisting of couches and sofas were spaced throughout the massive lounge. It made for easy, relaxed conversations among this large group of people.

Montoya had met Juan through the Oxonian Society. Despite its name, the society was not an Oxford alumni association, though the founders of the group were graduates of Oxford. Now called the Hudson Union Society, the group hosted talks featuring some of the world's most interesting minds, such as well-known writers, actors, journalists, politicians, and celebrities. Some were on book tours; others simply talked about their lives and work.

Both Juan and Montoya were Hudson Union Society patron members. This entitled them to meet the celebrity speakers in a private reception prior to an event, which is how they met. Juan had started inviting Montoya to his monthly poker nights at the Harvard Club of New York. Montoya reciprocated by inviting Juan to his many social events. The two of them kept busy social calendars, inviting each other back and forth.

"I can't believe that Juan was able to reserve both the rooftop and the main floor of 230 Fifth Avenue. There must be at least 1,500 people here," Tara said. "I see Juan trying to make the rounds to talk to everyone, but it seems like that would be impossible," Tara remarked to Nine, Frank, and Montoya.

Then, Montoya turned to Frank and asked, "So what do you think of her?" He smiled as he looked at a woman standing about twenty feet away from them.

"Pretty, but way too slutty," Frank replied as he looked over at the woman.

"So, how was your week, Frank?" Nine asked.

Frank sighed, "Working my ass off at my business. Meeting after meeting. We have this big sales campaign that needs to get ramped up and I've been working marathon hours. So, I can't stay out too late."

"Tara, are you seeing anyone these days?" Frank asked.

"Well, I went on a date with a guy named Liam. It was one of the worst dates of my life."

"What happened?" Frank inquired as he took a swig of his white wine.

"It was my first date with him. He took me to an expensive restaurant, but then when the bill came, he looked at me and said he forgot his wallet. What kind of guy invites you for a first date and then asks you to pay for it?"

"Unbelievable," Nine said.

"Yeah, so you know what I told him? 'I will bill you for your half.' "

"So, are you seeing him again?" Montoya asked teasing Tara.

"Funny!" Tara said with a sarcastic tone.

Just then, Juan made his way through the crowd to the group. Montoya caught Juan's attention and wished him a happy birthday as he shook his hand. Then he introduced Juan to Frank and Nine. Juan and Tara had met before so she also wished him a happy birthday and greeted him with a hug and kiss on his cheek.

"How do you like the party? Good people and good energy, right?" asked Juan.

"Definitely," Montoya responded.

"If you'll excuse me, I have to go over there and talk to some more people. Good seeing you!" Juan said as he turned and moved toward a small group of pretty women.

Tara glanced to her right, "Hey, Nine, that guy there is cute."

"You mean the one talking to the woman with the F cup?" Nine asked.

Frank cut into the conversation, "Those are huge! In case of a boating accident, she definitely won't drown."

"Bloody hell! Those might actually be a G or H cup," Montoya added.

"Oh stop!" Tara responded. "I've been told by some men that mine are pretty perky, although not in the F cup category."

Nine chimed in, "Mine are perky but only for Mr. Right."

Frank motioned to the left of Montoya, "Sorry to interrupt, but Montoya, look at those two women over there."

"You mean the real slutty ones?" Nine said making a joke.

"Funny. Not those two. The two to the right of them."

"Okay Frank," Montoya said, looking at the women, "They look good. Which one do you like?"

"As you know, I have my one-bullet theory like the character in the movie, *The Deer Hunter*. I only go for one woman per mixer. I want the brunette in the little black dress."

"That actually works out, because the other one seems more my type. So, ladies, we will return," Montoya said to Nine and Tara as he motioned to Frank.

"Have fun!" Nine said with a twinkle in her eye.

As Montoya and Frank walked across the room to talk to the two women, Juan's voice came over the loudspeakers thanking everyone for coming. Apparently, he had given up on trying to talk to everyone personally as he now spoke with a microphone. Then, a few of the lounge bar staff wheeled out a large birthday cake with candles on it for him.

Nine and Tara clapped as Juan blew out the candles. Tara pointed to a guy across the room and asked Nine, "What do you think of him? Oh, but we can't see his butt. Even if a guy is good looking, I know what matters to you."

"Yes, I'll admit that I am a 'good butt chaser.' But he also has to be tall. That guy looks a little too short."

"Yeah, tall is good. So, what exactly do you think is a good butt?"

"One that's like a butterball butt," Nine said laughing. "Firm, like in the military when you make your bed. It's a butt you could bounce a quarter off of."

A dark-haired man approached the two women. "Hi, my name is Gianni," he said in a thick Italian accent, "Are you friends with Juan?"

Nine looked over at Gianni noticing his day-old stubble. Not all men could rock that look, but on him it was definitely sexy. "I just met him through our friend Montoya," she told him.

"Montoya? Yes, I am friends with him also."

"Yeah, Montoya knows everyone," Tara added.

Turning toward Nine, Gianni leaned in close to whisper something in her ear.

"I am not sure I am that flexible, maybe I will be if I learn yoga," Nine said giggling.

A curvy brunette dressed in a loose-fitting blouse with a few too many buttons undone and a tight little black skirt approached the three of them. "I knew that I would find you with some pretty women," she said to Gianni. Then, giving a piercing look at Nine and Tara, she announced, "I am Luana, Gianni's girlfriend."

Seeing Luana's jealousy, Tara quickly responded, "We need to go find a few of our friends, nice to meet you though."

Nine and Tara walked away from Gianni and Luana. When they were out of earshot, Tara said to Nine, "I thought she was going to take out a gun and shoot you, the way she looked at you. I wouldn't want to get in the middle of that crossfire."

Nine responded, "It's pretty bad when your boyfriend hits on women right in front of you."

Nine noticed Tara shift her gaze, and both women looked over at Juan who now had a line of people waiting to wish him a happy birthday.

Meanwhile, Montoya and Frank had approached the two women Frank had pointed out earlier—a brunette and a blonde, who looked like they were in their late twenties.

Montoya opened the conversation with the blonde, "That is an interesting opal pendant. Can I see it closer?"

"Sure," the woman said, allowing Montoya to come closer to her.

Montoya picked up the pendant and started examining it but never looked down at her cleavage. "There's a lot of fire in that opal. It reflects what is in the wearer," he explained. "I'm Montoya and this is my friend Frank," he said extending his hand to shake hers.

The blonde woman wearing the opal pendant responded, "I am Jennifer and this is my friend Tawny."

"So, what do you do Montoya?" Jennifer asked.

"He's a magician," Frank said. "He works his magic."

"No, actually I am a lawyer."

"You ladies need to get on his social calendar," Frank added.

"Oh really? Why's that?" Tawny asked.

"He knows everything that is going on in this city and goes to a million social events," Frank continued.

"Maybe a tad less than a million, Frank. We don't want to get their expectations up too high."

"Impressive. So, you're a man in the know?" questioned Jennifer.

Taking this as a cue to be the perfect wingman by leaving Montoya to talk to Jennifer alone, Frank looked over at Tawny and asked, "Can I get you a drink?"

"Sure," Tawny responded.

While Frank and Tawny walked over to the bar, Montoya looked at Jennifer and asked, "Are you in school or do you work?"

Jennifer smiled but didn't answer.

"You could still be in graduate school," Montoya said returning her smile.

"Actually, I just got laid off from my consulting job."

"I'm sorry to hear that. What did you do for them?"

"I did project management." Then, she quickly changed the subject and asked, "What's the next big event on your social calendar?"

"I am having a party next week and you should come. I might not be able to get quite as many people as Juan, but you will meet a lot of people. Maybe you'll even make a connection to get a job."

"Sounds good."

Montoya reached into his pocket and said, "Here is my card. Do you have a card?"

"No, I'm unemployed remember?"

"No problem," Montoya added as he took out his wallet. "Here is a second card of mine. Write your email on the back of it. You can use my wallet to write on. But give the wallet back," he joked.

Jennifer wrote her email on the card.

"Write down your mobile number too."

Jennifer wrote down her number and then she handed the card and wallet back to Montoya. "From the accent, I am assuming you're British."

"Half-British and half-Spanish from Spain. I grew up in London which accounts for the accent."

"Which half is Spanish?"

"The bottom half," Montoya said playfully.

"I guess that means your father is Spanish?" Jennifer said playing along. "What is your last name?"

"Montoya is my last name."

"That is unusual. Just one name like Elvis or Madonna?"

"Well, I think it suits me better than my first name. My mother was a big fan of Cary Grant. His real name was Archibald Alexander Leach. So, my full name is Archibald Montoya. But I am not a big fan of Archibald or Archie for that matter. It is either associated with the television character Archie Bunker, or the comic book character, who hung around with Veronica, Betty, and Jughead. So, I just go by the one name of Montoya."

"I see. Actually, hearing the name 'Montoya,' makes me think of the movie, The Princess Bride, and that famous line 'You killed my father, prepare to die.' "

"It's a great movie. But as far as I know, my father is still alive, so you shouldn't be worried."

As Jennifer and Montoya talked, Frank got Tawny the drink he had promised her. As Tawny and Frank sipped their drinks, she asked, "Are you in fashion? You are such a sharp dresser."

"Fashion? No, but I do have a sense of style. The shirt goes on the top, the pants go on the bottom," Frank said dryly. "Seriously though, I own a few car dealerships." He handed Tawny his business card.

"Really, not one but a few car dealerships? That's impressive. My husband also owns a business," Tawny said.

"Your husband?!" Frank asked in surprise.

"Oh, I'm sorry, I meant my ex-husband. We are separated now and we're going to be divorced. The man was such a jerk. Cheated on me all the time," Tawny explained.

"Sorry to hear that. So, what do you do for a living?" Frank asked trying to change the subject.

"I mean he was just such a jerk. How did I not know that? Of course, we married after only half a year. I don't think you can really know someone in that short amount of time," Tawny continued.

Still trying to change the subject Frank said, "You do work right? What do you do for a living?"

"I mean, how do you really know if a guy is going to cheat on you? A good man is so hard to find. He was great in bed. Always hard. It was like he was always on Viagra even though he didn't need it since he was the same age as me. I guess a hard man is also a good find, but I guess I wasn't enough for him. I was devastated when I realized that he was cheating on me."

Jennifer and Montoya came over and interrupted Tawny's monologue. Jennifer looked at her watch and said, "We actually have to go to another party. Tawny, are you ready to go?"

"Yes, I'm ready. Frank, I'll text you sometime," Tawny said as she held up Frank's business card.

"Without a doubt," Frank responded.

Montoya kissed Jennifer on the cheek. "I will see you next week at my party."

"Wow! Do you kiss every woman you've just met?"

"Just the pretty ones," Montoya responded.

"So, you really are a charmer, huh? See you next week."

"As you wish," Montoya said with a sly smile.

"Funny," Jennifer said as she turned to head out with Tawny.

Montoya looked at Frank as the women walked away. "So?"

"Not happening," Frank responded.

"Why? You seemed to be really into her. She is totally your type."

"She spent the whole time complaining about her husband."

"She's married?"

"She is separated and she is going through a divorce right now. She was going on and on about how bad the guy was," Frank explained.

"With women, it's important to be a good listener. I have a lot of women in my life because I've learned that when a woman wants to talk, just listen. That's all they want, someone to listen."

"If I could, I'd like to pick and choose what I have to listen to. I have to deal with enough crap at work. I don't need to hear more from someone else going on and on about her problems," Frank said.

"I'm telling you Frank. Women like good listeners. Almost as much as they like multiple orgasms."

"So, I will only give them half of what they want," Frank said as he chuckled.

"Let's go check up on Tara and Nine," Montoya said to Frank. "Unless you want me to be your wingman for somebody else."

"No, Merlin. I'm done for the night," Frank said. "I'm not an Uzi machine gun like you—approaching multiple women. I just have my one bullet."

At that moment, a curvaceous brunette approached Montoya and Frank. "Hey I have been watching you two. You're both pretty smooth operators. I'm Luana Cruz."

Montoya looked over at Luana recognizing her. She was a stunner with olive-colored skin, hazel eyes, and long dark hair. "You probably don't remember me, but I already met you once before when you were with Gianni," Montoya said as he shook her hand.

"My boyfriend is coming on to anyone who has tits at this party! Hopefully you aren't like him!"

Montoya replied, "No, definitely not."

"Hey!" Luana ignored Montoya and turned to Frank, "I have a boyfriend but I am free on Mondays and Thursdays."

Frank was not paying much attention, but just then, he looked over at her. She was obviously a knockout. Her short skirt showed off her toned legs and butt. She was quite sexy but something about her approach annoyed him.

"Look, I'm not interested in being anyone's two-day a week sex toy. Sorry, but not interested," Frank said as he walked away to find Tara and Nine.

"You can dress him up but can't take him anywhere," Montoya remarked.

"Who cares!" she said as she downed the remainder of her drink.

"Hey, try to save some liquor for the rest of us. It seems like you've had more than enough for the night."

"I haven't drunk that much!"

"I don't know, but you're starting to sway back and forth, which would be fine if you were on a cruise ship, but you're on dry land my dear. Maybe I should look for Gianni to help get you home."

"Who gives a crap what that SOB is doing? He's probably screwing someone in some dark corner right now."

"Didn't mean to get you upset but maybe I should take you home."

"I don't need a babysitter," Luana said as she grabbed Montoya's wine and downed it. "Hey, there are plenty of pretty women here for you. Look at that one. She could be your future ex-wife," she said laughing at her own joke.

Luana walked away teetering precariously in her heels and approached another guy, "Hey, I'm thinking of taking you home tonight. What's your name?"

The guy looked down her blouse and got a glimpse of her nipples since she was not wearing a bra. "My name is Brian. So, you're taking me home tonight?!" he said enthusiastically.

Montoya stepped between Brian and Luana, "Actually, I wouldn't get your hopes up too high."

That last drink that Luana had gulped down seemed to be kicking in as she draped her arm around Montoya, and leaned on him as she tried to steady herself.

"Who the hell are you?" Brian responded with annoyance in his voice.

"Her brother! Luana, I am taking you home," Montoya said firmly. "Excuse me!" He put his arm around Luana and pulled her away from Brian. "Let's go."

As they turned and walked away, Brian yelled, "Hey! I didn't get your name. What is your number?"

Montoya yelled back at Brian, "She doesn't have a number!" He continued to escort Luana out of the lounge as she struggled to put one step in front of the other. After exiting the building he held Luana and supported her as he hailed a cab. When a cab pulled up, he opened the door for her, helped her in, and sat next to her.

"Where are we going?!" Luana asked loudly.

"Yeah, pal, where are you going?" the cab driver asked.

"I am bringing you home." Montoya reached into her pocketbook and pulled out her driver's license and then told the driver, "81st and Third Avenue."

Then, he pulled out his phone and texted Frank, Tara, Nine, and Juan, telling them that he had to leave the party early and was sorry that he couldn't say goodbye.

Back at 230 Fifth, Juan's birthday party was still going full swing. Nine's on-again off-again boyfriend Paul had showed up. Tara knew that Paul had recently gone MIA on Nine and sensed that the two of them needed to sort out some things. So, Tara left them alone to talk and she walked around to circulate.

"Hey, Tara! How have you been?" Tara turned to see Mike, one of the most jovial and congenial people she knew. They had gone to the same college. She had met him at one of the Asian Student

Association meetings that she had attended during her freshman year at Brown University.

"Hi Mike. I haven't seen you in ages. How do you know Juan?"

"I don't, but I think that my friend who invited me does, or someone he knows, does."

"Yeah, how is it possible to have more than a thousand close friends? I don't know how he does it. He certainly knows how to get a crowd. It really is pretty impressive that all of these people ended up here to celebrate his birthday!"

"So, is everything good? Are you still working at the same place these days?"

"Yes, what about you?"

"I'm still working at the American Cancer Society. Thanks for being such a faithful donor all these years since graduating from college."

"Yes, I'm glad that I was able to help out the first year that you were there. Every year since I've chosen a different cancer-related cause to raise money for. Last year, I organized a group to do the breast cancer walk in Central Park and the year before that I helped organize a Relay For Life event."

"This year I'm working on a different sort of fundraising event and we're still looking for people to volunteer," Mike said.

"Oh that's great! What's the new event? I'd be happy to help out."

"Well, yes, maybe you can help us out. This year we are doing something really fun. We are going to have a date auction and I'm going to be the emcee!" Mike explained.

"Oh! Are you asking me to auction myself off? I'm not going to have to walk down a runway or do a little twirl, will I?" Tara asked.

"No, nothing like that. Just look beautiful, like you always do, and may the highest bidder win!"

"Ha ha! Why does the movie Indecent Proposal suddenly come to mind? But what if things backfire? I'd be at the mercy of the whims of the bidders."

"Don't worry. I'll be there. It's all in good fun," Mike said with a wink.

"I'm not so sure about this, but since it's for charity, I'll consider enduring the public scrutiny. You know how to reach me," Tara said.

While Tara and Mike bantered, the cab with Luana and Montoya drove by the upscale boutiques of Madison Avenue. Luana rested her head on Montoya's shoulder and said, "So, you want to kick the tires with me? Do a test drive?"

"No, Luana, I am your friend tonight. I will make sure you get home safely."

"You want to help me put on my pajamas? Tuck me in?"

"It is tempting."

She put her hand on his lap. "If I rub this, will the genie come out and play with me?" Luana asked giggling.

Montoya removed her hand from his lap. "Not tonight. If you were not tipsy and didn't have a boyfriend, yes, Luana, I would totally make out with you and maybe more. But tonight you are pissed drunk. It would be really taking advantage of you and I won't do that."

The taxi arrived at Luana's address and Montoya paid the cabbie. Luana was very wobbly, so Montoya helped her out of the car. He opened the door and as they walked into the lobby, the doorman stopped him. Luana muttered, "It's okay, he's just helping me home." The doorman said, "Eighth floor, apartment 8C sir." They walked over to the elevators and into one that was waiting with its doors wide open. Montoya pressed the eighth floor to get up to her apartment. By now, Luana was barely conscious so Montoya reached into her pocketbook to get her keys. Once they made it to her apartment, he opened the door, scanned the layout of the apartment and saw the door to the bedroom ajar. He took Luana to the bedroom and placed her down gently on the bed and took off her heels. As Montoya pulled the covers over her, Luana whispered, "I want me... you... me inside me."

"I think you mean you want me inside you." Montoya kissed her on the forehead, "Maybe another time, if you weren't with Gianni, but not tonight." He then placed one of his business cards on the bedside table.

Luana had already fallen fast asleep, so he walked out of her bedroom, and closed the door. As he walked out of the front door, he locked it before leaving. Then he left Luana's keys downstairs with the doorman.

Meanwhile, back at Juan's birthday party, Frank had finally found Tara. "Any luck tonight?" he inquired.

"Maybe. I just gave my card to a cute guy about ten minutes ago. What about you, Frank?" Tara responded.

"No luck tonight. Tried it with that brunette I pointed to earlier, but that isn't going to happen. I'm ready to head out."

"Me too. Did you see the text from Montoya?" Tara asked. "It sounds like he had some drama tonight."

"Nothing he can't handle. I am positive about that," Frank said as he saw Nine in the distance talking to Paul. "Knowing how Nine and Paul can get, should we just leave them to it, and wave goodbye to her on the way out? I have a meeting in the morning and they might be here a long time."

"You're right about that," Tara said and they walked to the elevator. They waved goodbye to Nine as they passed her.

Nine waved back as she continued talking. It looked as if she and Paul had gotten into another one of their arguments.

"Nine, I really care about you, but we keep arguing over the same issue. You keep wanting me to move to New York, but I can't right now. My job is in the Bay Area. We keep trying to make it work long distance, but it doesn't seem to be working out."

"I know, Paul."

"I am okay seeing you once or twice a month. But you don't seem to be happy with that."

"I really don't like it that you don't want to be exclusive anymore. It's like our relationship is going backwards," Nine declared.

"I'm sorry Nine. But I can't be in an exclusive relationship with you if I'm 3,000 miles away. We keep going round and round on this. I think that maybe this should be my last trip to New York for a while. I think we should take a break and see where we go from here."

"I can't believe this is it, but it just seems like it isn't meant to be," she acknowledged wiping away a tear that ran down her cheek.

Paul kissed Nine on the lips and put his arm around her shoulder. "Let me take you to the street level and hail you a cab."

"No, it's alright." She looked at Paul sadly and reached over to hug him. "Let this be our goodbye here." She gave him a quick kiss on the lips, walked to the elevator and got in, giving Paul one last wave goodbye.

Postscript: Juan, the one-man networking machine, has since moved to Miami where he's started a new life, but New York City misses him.

Knowing and Not Knowing

(TARA)

My friend Minh and I were sitting at a trendy hotel bar in the Flatiron District, deeply engaged in conversation about everything from dealing with the health issues of our aging parents to celebrity sightings. We were discussing "big love" and that undeniable feeling, when the relationship just seems right.

We talked about how big love is not to be mistaken for larger-than-life love, which is just so unhealthy. Larger-than-life love is like a sinkhole—it just takes over everything, throwing reason out the window, leaving you in a constant state of yearning and dissatisfaction, and feeling as if it is never enough.

Minh was telling me about this guy David, who she had just met at an Asian Young Professionals (AYP) event, a social networking organization for single Asians. We were definitely getting a little too engrossed in deep conversation for a Friday night. It was the end of another workweek, which should've meant that it was time to just kick back and relax.

A man standing at the bar and right beside me waiting for his drink looked over at us and introduced himself. "Hi, I'm Matt. Where are you ladies from?"

I had noticed him. He had dark brown hair and a clean-cut look. The bartender brought Matt a scotch on the rocks. Minh and I looked at each other. "Well, I'm not sure how to answer that. But I'd say I'm a New Yorker. I've lived here for several years now," I offered.

Matt set his drink down on the bar beside mine. "Well, I've lived in Connecticut, New York, Southern California, and Colorado. But I'm Irish. My grandparents actually came over here from Ireland."

Minh looked over at Matt and said, "I'm from Hoi An in central Vietnam. I came here a few years ago to get my MBA."

Straight to the point, and always very direct, Minh knows who she is, I thought.

Matt turned to me and asked, "So, what about you? I'm not sure how to ask this…" Matt's voice trailed off as he looked at me, "But where are you from? I mean what's your family background?"

I smiled and asked, "Why don't you take a guess?"

"Well, I don't think you're Chinese… but maybe Thai, or Filipino?"

"Hmmm… close… I think I'll leave you guessing," I said in a sprightly way.

I thought to myself that the truth is, I didn't exactly know where I was from. When my birth mother had shown up with me, then a three-month-old baby at an orphanage in Thailand, she didn't have any identification with her. Though she could speak Thai, something about the way that she spoke made workers at the orphanage guess that she may have been a refugee who had escaped out of Cambodia.

As an adult, I learned that the orphanage had close ties with Thai human rights organizations and activists who helped Cambodians who were fleeing from the wrath of the Khmer Rouge. Thailand was the gateway to freedom for many Cambodian refugees, even years after the fall of Pol Pot. All my birth mother had told the orphanage was that her baby girl was named Chantara, and was born in the fourth month of the Khmer calendar. Because of that, the date of birth on my documents is a guesstimate and I don't know the exact date of my birth.

My exact country of origin remains a mystery even now because my given name, Chantara, is both a Cambodian and a Thai name. In Khmer it means moon and stars, whereas in Thai it means moon and water. My adoptive parents had brought me over to the United States from Thailand and raised me in Connecticut. Growing up, no one knew exactly how to pronounce my name, so I just decided to make things easier and to go by the name of Tara.

Matt broke my train of thought. "Well, my ex-girlfriend was from Thailand. People from Thailand, they are good people. I met her parents and they were the sweetest people."

"So, what happened to her, your ex?" Minh chimed in.

"Oh, she was kind of young and immature. What about you two ladies? What are the two of you doing here? Just the two of you?"

Minh took one last sip of her martini and set it down, "Well, I am kind of with someone."

Matt leaned over and looked at Minh and me with a raised eyebrow.

"Oh, I know what you're thinking. We are not with each other. The two of us," I pointed from Minh to myself, "We are not together!"

Matt's phone rang and he reached into his pocket to answer it. "Yeah, I'm still here. It's at the corner of Park Avenue and 28th Street. Sure, come on over," he said to the person on the other end.

Minh and I looked at each other, and we knew it was time to call it a night. Matt hung up his phone.

"Well, it's time to move on now. We've got to meet up with some other friends uptown," Minh announced.

"It was so nice meeting you girls. Too bad you're not sticking around. One of my buddies is on his way over," Matt said as Minh and I put on our jackets.

Outside on the sidewalk, the two of us laughed.

Minh spoke first, "Isn't that always when it happens—right when you're taken or getting involved with someone, that's when some handsome guy tries to pick you up!"

"Well, it looks as if you are really into this new guy you told me about. It seems like human nature, that when you're taken, somehow men know this and then you somehow seem even more attractive to them." Seeing Minh eyeing the street for a cab, I told her, "It's always so great catching up with you!" Minh hailed a cab, then we hugged before she got in.

As I walked home, I thought about how it must be nice to be the sort of person who knows exactly who she is, where she's from, where she's going, and what she wants to do, like Minh. In the past when people have asked and tried to guess my ethnic background, I usually played along. It was just easier. They guessed Thai, Singaporean, Taiwanese, Filipino, Vietnamese, Chinese—you name it. If it's been guessed, I've played the part. I'm really not entirely sure if I am Thai or Cambodian.

It was a short walk home and soon I was in my apartment. I glanced at a photograph of my adoptive parents displayed on one of the bookshelves in my living room as I walked into my bedroom to get ready for bed. It was my favorite photograph of them taken in Thailand. That's where they had met, when both were there on Rotary Peace Fellowships. After returning to the United States together and several years of marriage, they discovered that they were not able to have children. So, they decided to go back to Thailand to see if they could find a child to adopt.

My parents did their best to help me understand my roots. While growing up, they had told me about the shared history of Thailand and Cambodia. As a teenager I'd watched *The Killing Fields* with my parents, and the topic of Cambodia's war-torn past had come up. Looking back on it now, perhaps it was a way for my parents to bring up a discussion on this topic with me.

They had several albums of gorgeous photos from their time in Southeast Asia. As a child, I would flip through the albums imagining my parents in this faraway land, posing for photos. My favorite photos were those of Thai and Cambodian traditional dancers. Their elaborate headpieces and jewelry captured my imagination, but I could never tell which was Thai and which was Cambodian. Both cultures seemed quite similar. My parents had told me that both had roots in Khmer culture.

Throughout my childhood, my mother Angela, would periodically prepare traditional Cambodian and Thai dishes for me. My favorite was khao thom, which is a rice soup that's eaten with pickled vegetables, fermented soy beans, and leftovers. I knew that all of this was a part of my heritage, but I had never been back to Asia since I'd been adopted at the age of three.

A Beautiful Friendship

(MONTOYA and Luana)

One warm spring afternoon, I walked across the street to Marseille on Restaurant Row in the Times Square District. It was an unpretentious, spacious and elegant restaurant. As soon as I entered, I saw where Luana was seated. She waved when she saw me and I made my way to her. I greeted her by shaking her hand and kissing her on the cheek in one simultaneous motion. Then, we both sat down and surveyed the menu.

"So, who are you really? And what were you before? What did you do and what did you think?" I asked Luana facetiously.

"*Casablanca* right? Great movie. But how did you know I would catch the reference?" Luana responded.

"I get the strong feeling that you are a romantic."

"I am, although most people think I am a flirt," Luana said dryly.

"As the old expression goes... it takes one to know one. I am a romantic and a flirt also."

After ordering our food and over the course of our conversation, I discovered that Luana was quite smart. She had attended some of the best boarding schools in Europe. Her undergraduate degree was from Stanford in statistics, and she also had a master's degree and a Ph.D. in physics from Yale University. She had used her Ph.D. in physics to get a job as a top financial analyst on Wall Street. I realized that due to her educational background she didn't speak English with a traditional Brazilian accent.

"I'm very glad you called me for lunch. I wanted to know that you were okay after the other night," I told her.

"You've given me hope that there are still some nice guys in New York. I really want to thank you for taking care of me. I was a drunken mess the other night and you were great. Really great," Luana said reaching to touch my hand.

"I know that Gianni seems to have a wandering eye. Sorry about that."

"He would have sex with anyone female. She could be old or ugly, it wouldn't matter to him. I have never felt comfortable having any of my women friends around him," Luana responded.

"How many times has he cheated on you?"

"That I know of? At least thirty times."

"Thirty times?! Why in the world are you still with him?"

"Hey, I thought you were Gianni's friend? Aren't you going to stick up for him?" Luana asked.

"No. I've been thinking about this for a while. I like Gianni, but he's more of an acquaintance than a friend. The cheating thing is quite bad. I really don't want to be guilty by association."

"Interesting. So, you really are a nice guy."

"I'd like to think I am a decent guy, not necessarily a nice guy."

"What's the difference?"

"As I said earlier, I am a flirt also, actually, a notorious flirt. But I have a code of ethics I follow. I don't cheat."

"So, you have a girlfriend?"

"Been on again and off again with someone who is driving me crazy. Her name is Evelyn. All my friends say I should move on."

"Sounds like we are in the same boat. I have tried to break up with Gianni many times and I keep going back to him."

"Why?"

The waitress brought our food but I was more interested in hearing Luana's line of reasoning than the food.

"I love his body. He is also the best lover I've ever had. He knocks on my door at three in the morning. When I tell him to go away, he keeps knocking until I let him in. I don't want him to wake up the neighbors. Then, I yell and scream at him."

"I am assuming you screaming and yelling at three in the morning would annoy the neighbors also?"

"Yes, it does but guys like him take all that yelling and then afterwards he says he is sorry and we have sex again. This has happened over and over. For three years I have been trying to break up with him."

"Three years? Bugger! I have only known him half a year. Let me ask you a dumb question. Why not report him to the police when he knocks on your door? If you have a doorman, tell him not to let Gianni up."

"Are you serious? You are taking my side?"

"I have been thinking about this ever since I met Gianni. I don't think it's right what he is doing to all these women, and especially to you."

"After a while, I actually didn't even know if I could say that I was the one that he was cheating on. You do know he is technically still married, right?"

"Are you serious? I didn't know that."

"He is separated, but not divorced. So, these past three years, he was technically cheating on his wife with me. Although they are no longer living under the same roof, I'm not so sure just how 'separated' they actually are. So, the crazy thought is, am I the one he is cheating with or the one he is cheating on? Because there have been other women besides me."

"You need to set boundaries and take control of the situation for yourself. I mean he cheated on you over thirty times. So, now, you need to do something drastic that gets his attention."

"Right, I want to put a stop to this," Luana said with conviction.

"Well, I have never suggested this to anyone before, but this is an exception. You should check out this website where women post about men who they want to warn other women about. I know someone who did this to her ex-husband because he cheated on her. Put him on it and it will definitely get his attention."

"Oh really? Can you write that down for me?" Luana asked as she handed me a piece of paper and pen from her purse.

"Sure," I said as I took the pen and started writing the website's address on the piece of paper.

"Tell me, what happened with your friend whose ex-husband was cheating on her?" Luana asked with curiosity.

"Well, that's what led to him becoming her ex-husband. There was no turning back for them after that," I explained.

"I didn't have a cheating ex-husband, but I have been divorced for other reasons."

"Do you mind if I ask what happened?" I inquired as I returned the pen and paper to her.

"We had been together for a few years when I unexpectedly got pregnant. We were so happy about it because we had talked about having a family and it's what we both wanted. So, we got married immediately and started planning for our family. But then, I had a miscarriage at three months."

"I'm sorry to hear that," I said.

"It was devastating. I wasn't sure if I wanted to try again right away, but about a year later, I got pregnant again. Miguel was overjoyed but I was more cautiously optimistic. I didn't want to tell anyone until I was in the second trimester," Luana explained and then paused.

"I see," I said waiting for Luana to continue.

"It was a girl, Marisol. When she came into our lives, everything changed forever. And, then, one day, just like that, she was gone," Luana said recalling the sad memory. "It was sudden infant death syndrome."

"I'm really sorry to hear that you went through that," I said as I put my hand on Luana's.

"It now seems like a lifetime ago. The marriage was just not the same after that. I was the one who found her," Luana said getting choked up as her eyes welled up with tears.

"We don't have to continue talking about this if it's too upsetting," I said as I reached into my pocket and handed Luana a handkerchief.

Luana dabbed her eyes with the handkerchief and said, "No, no, it's okay. I feel I can share this with you. So… after that, the nursery became a painful reminder for me. I wanted to redecorate and repaint it, but Miguel couldn't bring himself to do it. He didn't pressure me about trying again, but even though he didn't say it, his actions told me that's what he wanted eventually."

"You obviously needed time to heal, but Miguel didn't see that?" I asked.

"At the time, I might have felt that way, but I now realize that we just had different ways of dealing with grief."

"Did you want to have a kid with Gianni?"

"When I met Gianni three years ago at a party, and I had been divorced for a while. I was in a better place and had thought about one day trying to have a child again. I did think about having a baby with Gianni, but now I realize that he is so irresponsible and immature. If I had a kid with him, it would be like having two kids.

I'm not sure he could handle the responsibility of being a father. Although, you never really know how someone is going to be when the child, their child actually arrives. But with men in New York, you have to keep it a secret that you want a baby. That makes them run away."

"Nobody wants to feel like they are being used and for men, the four biggies that we are used for are money, sex, citizenship, and sperm," I explained.

"Sperm?"

"What I mean is when a woman wants you more for the ability to give her a baby than for being her boyfriend or husband."

"I want the whole package. The sperm, the dick, and the baby," Luana said cheekily as she handed the handkerchief back to me.

I realized that her mood had improved and then I said, "You mean the sperm, the penis, and the baby? You don't want a dick." Luana laughed upon hearing this and then I added, "I think you deserve a good guy."

"Thanks for your advice. I'll keep you posted."

The waitress came over with the check. Luana immediately grabbed it. "This one is definitely on me."

"Remember the last scene from the movie *Casablanca*?"

"Very funny!" Luana said understanding what I was referring to.

"Yes, Luana, this is the beginning of a beautiful friendship," I said with a warm smile.

Missionary Dating

(NINE)

I am very committed to being a Christian, but my world isn't black and white, which is kind of ironic for me to say since I really am half black (that's my father's side) and half white (that's my mother's side). My dad is African-American while my mom is German, which gives me dual citizenship—American and German. I've been blessed with the best of both of my parents' genes. I have my dad's height and my mother's green eyes. People can't always tell what my ethnicity is. Sometimes, it's fun to have them try to guess.

My parents met at the Nienburg Abbey, a thousand-year-old Benedictine monastery in the town of Nienburg, in the Saxony Anhalt area of Germany. At the time, my dad was stationed at Ramstein Air Force Base in Germany as an Air Force Lieutenant Colonel. My father, James, has always been fascinated with old churches, so he decided to visit the abbey, while on leave. My mother, Astrid, was a tour guide there, and my father ended up in her group—that's how they met.

A few months later, my father proposed and they arranged to get married at the abbey. I was born in Germany and my parents decided to name me after the town where they met and were wed. We lived at Ramstein Air Force Base and then Spangdahlem Air Force Base (also in Germany) until I turned eight, which accounts for my fluency in German. Then, my father was promoted and we moved to MacDill Air Force Base in Tampa, Florida. We kept moving around to different bases, both in the U.S. and abroad until we finally wound up at Scott Air Force Base in Illinois.

I've always thought that the intent behind my name was romantic. But when I started going to school in the U.S., it wasn't fun being teased about it. The kids at school thought, what kind of a name is Nienburg for a girl? Later on, I adopted the nickname "Nine." Surprisingly, my nickname has kind of worked in my favor. Introducing myself as Nine to guys, has often resulted in some very interesting reactions, which is not a bad thing at all.

Looking at my parents' marriage and relationship, that's what I want, but dating for a Christian woman like me has never been easy in New York. Even with all of the churches here, you would think that it would be easy to find a good guy. But it wasn't always like this. The church I've been attending for the past three years, The Journey Church, was one of the first churches in Manhattan that was "cool" and attracted people my age. It's a contemporary church that opens its services with a live rock music band performance. Now, even with many other churches in Manhattan similar to The Journey, it's still tough.

My problem is that I am looking for the trifecta in Christian dating. He has to be cool, cute, and Christian—the three C's. I guess tall would also be a requirement. Most guys would be cool and not cute, or cute and not cool, or cute and cool but not tall. I know this makes me sound a bit like Goldilocks—constantly saying this porridge is too hot or this porridge is too cold—but so far I haven't been able to find the porridge that is just right. I did come close once with Paul, who I met at a fundraiser in Midtown for Howard University. We started a long distance relationship since he was based in San Francisco and working on a startup. He was indeed cool, cute and Christian.

I knew how passionate Paul was about the startup and I admired his ambition. The idea of living in New York appealed to him. He had said he'd love to live in New York one day. That was the long-term plan, but he wanted to get the startup off the ground first. Over time I saw him less and less frequently and our relationship became on again and off again. Then Paul said he couldn't be exclusive with me anymore. That's when I realized that things had changed and we were not on such solid ground anymore.

After it didn't work out with Paul, who actually had the three C's, I decided to go back to what is known as "missionary dating." That is, I dated guys who weren't Christian. In doing so, I hoped that somehow my great looks and dazzling personality (and of course my humility, just kidding) would get them interested in attending my church. The idea was that they'd eventually consider Christianity as a way to get to know me better.

Before Paul there was Kurt, who was German and a lapsed Lutheran. He had stopped going to church in his freshman year at college. But after dating me, he started attending The Journey Church. We were together for two months, but then I started to get this weird feeling that somehow he knew things that he could only know by reading my emails. After I got into a fight with him, I would write out my feelings in an email, but I never sent the email, and just kept it saved as a draft. I'd look at what I'd written down from time to time and after a while I would delete it.

Kurt always seemed to know the right things to ask me, and what to apologize for after our arguments. This made me suspicious. So, I decided to do a test. I told a girlfriend that I would be sending her a bogus email and for her not to respond. In the bogus email, I said that I was having an affair with someone else behind Kurt's back.

It didn't take long for Kurt to call and start probing me. Eventually, he started accusing me of having an affair with someone else. I told him that I'd specifically written about the affair in the email as a test and sent it my friend. I told him that none of it was true and, then, I also asked him how he could possibly know about the email. He knew that he had been caught so he confessed that he had been aware of my email password for almost the entire time we were together. I was furious and told him that not only had he violated my privacy but also the privacy of all my friends, since he was reading their emails to me as well. So, things ended abruptly with him.

More recently, there was this guy at work, Yves, who I had a major flirtation with. Our first date was brunch together and he attended The Journey Church three times. Yves was a little on the short side, but that didn't stop me from making out with him from time to time. He was a good guy, though he seemed to be too controlling for me. Then, I found out from a co-worker that he already had a girlfriend in Paris and that he was waiting for her to come back to New York City. So, I decided that I really didn't want to be any guy's plan B or filler until the real girlfriend returned.

Then, The Journey Church did a sermon series on dating and they weren't so keen on missionary dating. They may have a point because it hasn't been working out for me anyway.

The Dancer

(MONTOYA)

Jennifer and I were eating at Ooki Sushi, a Japanese restaurant on the Upper East Side sitting adjacent to each other at a corner table.

"Thanks again for inviting me to your party last month. That's how I met Bentley, who as you know, works for a foreign bank. He contacted me and I have an interview this coming Friday. I'm so glad that you introduced yourself to me at Juan's party," Jennifer said.

"My pleasure," I responded.

"So, are you as good with relationships as you are with setting people up for job opportunities?" Jennifer asked.

"You'd have to ask the women I've been with if I am good at relationships. However, I would definitely say that I am good at dating. While my friends would say that I'm a flirt, I do try to be a gentleman."

"So, you help women with their coats, pull out a chair, or open doors for them?"

"Yes, among other things," I said suggestively.

"What type of woman are you looking for?" Jennifer inquired.

"I want a woman who will value the intimacy and friendship of a relationship. Even after breaking up, I've stayed friends with every single one of my ex-girlfriends, except the love of my life."

"Why is that?" Jennifer asked.

"Oh, that's kind of a long story. I don't think you want to hear all about that on a first date."

"No, it's ok. I want to get to know you better."

"It was a long time ago, when I was at uni."

"Oh, we were all young and foolish at one time. You go first and then I'll tell you about the love of my life," Jennifer said reassuring me.

"Ok, I'll hold you to that," I said looking at Jennifer. "I met her as a freshman at Oxford. Her name was Jane and I had fallen so hard for her. She was the love of my life and the first person I had ever fallen in love with. However she felt that I was smothering her."

"Uh-huh," Jennifer said nodding.

"The relationship was on and off for two years. After each break-up, I'd desperately want to get back together with her. It was like Jane was a drug and I couldn't handle the withdrawal symptoms."

"Oh, I know how that can be."

"Finally, one day, Jane just stopped returning my calls, and disappeared. She literally ran away from me, and I was devastated. After the breakup, I brooded and brooded over how not to repeat the mistakes I had made with Jane," I said.

"And so you never ever heard from her again?" Jennifer asked.

"No, I never did hear from her again."

"I think that after a breakup, it's hard not to look back and think about the mistakes you've made and what you could've done differently," Jennifer commented.

"I rationalized that Jane had a fear of commitment, but after brooding on it so much, I came to a revelation of sorts. Her fear of commitment and, I think this is true for most people, was really a fear of losing her personal identity, and needing her freedom and personal space," I continued.

"I think that maybe for men, it is a little different and the fear of commitment is really a fear of being controlled,"

Jennifer paused for a moment and then continued. "You seem like a decent man and it sounds like Jane was somewhat heartless. As I look back at some of the men who I've dated, I've asked myself: how did I ever date that jerk or dirtbag?"

"You are spot on. Many of us have said to ourselves: 'How could I have been so stupid?' or 'Why didn't I see it?' or 'What was I thinking?' " I responded.

"I can really relate. So, here's my story. I was on again, off again, with a guy for the past year. He was an actor and was working at a small wine bar in the East Village. But during the day, he was always out on auditions. I went to all his readings and off-off Broadway shows and even read lines with him late at night, at the end of his wait shift."

"I actually know many actors and actresses because I've been volunteering for a small not-for-profit theater and film company to learn the ropes. I've always wanted to be a screenwriter and to produce movies from my own scripts. I am afraid to ask what his name is since I just might know him," I said.

"Trevor McGee."

"I think I might have seen his headshot somewhere, but I've never met him."

"He definitely has the looks of a leading man, and that's why I fell for him so quickly. I told him I loved him after three months and he seemed to want me as his girlfriend, but he never said it back. Every time I showed any real interest in him, he would back up and find ways to distance himself. But then, when I would start to back up, he would come forward saying that he really wanted a relationship. Each time he was entirely convincing, but somehow he'd end up backing away again."

"Actually, I have come up with a name for this type. I would say that Trevor is a 'dancer type.' "

"What is a 'dancer type?' " Jennifer asked.

"The 'dancer' only feels comfortable when you are not serious in the relationship. Jane was a dancer type. If you get serious and want to take the relationship to a higher level, the dancer type moves back. If you move back, then they come forward, sort of like a dance. I believe that these types of people do want to be in a relationship, but they are in denial of the fact that they are actually commitment-phobic."

"Why are you such an expert on this?"

"Because I just got out of a relationship with another 'dancer type.' Her name is Evelyn and we did this back-and-forth dance like I just described. She was totally focused on making it as an investment banker and never had any time for me," I explained.

"So, were you in love with these two women you mentioned?" Jennifer asked.

"Yes, I was. I have been deeply in love three times."

"Really?"

"The first was with Jane when I was in uni, the second one was when I was in my twenties and now Evelyn."

"How long did things go on with Evelyn?" Jennifer asked.

"Six months."

"And how did it end?"

"After all this going back and forth, I realized that I was feeling the same withdrawal symptoms that I had felt with Jane. It took a while for it to register, but I realized that I was in love with Evelyn because she reminded me of Jane, my first love."

"And how long ago was that?"

"It was about a month ago. What really helped me to get over it was helping out a woman friend of mine who had trouble with her boyfriend who is a notorious cheater. After seeing her follow my advice, I thought I should practice what I preach. So, I finally ended it."

"Good for you!"

"Evelyn recently contacted me, but I knew she wasn't the right person for me and I told her that I just wanted to be friends. She was shocked that I didn't want to continue the dance and tried to get me to change my mind, but I stuck to my guns."

Jennifer looked down at the table and was silent for a few moments.

"Is anything wrong?" I asked.

"I'm sorry to say this Montoya. You are a great guy. But listening to you, I have to admit that I am still in love with Trevor. I don't think I could start a relationship with anyone."

"I realize we got into a heavy conversation for a first date," I said.

"I know, but this conversation makes me recognize I still have really strong feelings for him."

"It's sad to say, but I think people really have to hit rock bottom with a 'dancer type' before they can decide it's over and move on," I asserted.

Postscript: I later learned that Jennifer went back to Trevor and they were married six months after her date with me. They were divorced three months after that because he cheated on her. When she demanded to know why he cheated, his answer was that she was smothering him.

The Date Auction

(FRANK and Tara)

It isn't every day that a woman tells you that she's going to be up for sale to the highest bidder. Tara had gotten involved in a charity event organized by the Asian Americans for Hope to benefit the American Cancer Society, and this year their fundraiser was to be a date auction.

Tara seemed a bit anxious about it, having asked me, "What if no one bids on me?" or "What if I only get a really low bid? Or worse yet, what if some weirdo bids on me?"

I knew that although she was normally self-confident, her mind seemed to be going into overdrive regarding this. The fear of being embarrassed and humiliated seemed to drive Tara's insistence that I come to the event as her protector. My job was to be there to drive up the bidding and to save her from being forced to go on a date with some creepy, questionable guy. She was asking me to spend my hard-earned cash on her to spare her from embarrassment. The things you do for friendship. But I also knew that the money would be going to a worthy cause since I had an aunt who had lost her battle with breast cancer less than two years ago.

The auction took place at a restaurant on the Lower East Side. What most of the restaurant patrons that day did not know was that in the lower level, men and women were waiting nervously to be auctioned off. Think about it. When you get down to it, literally putting yourself out there to have a price tag stamped on you is not an easy thing to do. You've got to take it in stride, and try not to take any of it too personally or seriously.

As I walked into the room I saw Tara immediately. She was dressed in a loose-fitting purple dress that managed to hug her curves and show off her slim figure without being too revealing.

"Hey Frank," she said waving at me looking a bit nervous.

I walked over and kissed her on the cheek, "So, how much is this going to wind up costing me?"

Tara looked a little more relaxed, "Come on Frank, you know how much I really appreciate your being here for me and doing this. It's all for a good cause."

I was glad to see her more at ease. I paused and looked around. It was a full house, with a quite impressive turnout. The room held a lot of attractive women. The men, I was not so sure about.

A man dressed in a dark suit and a red tie got on the microphone and started to quiet down the crowd. "Good afternoon, everyone! My name is Mike. How is everybody doing today?" The crowd quickly quieted down as Mike continued, "On behalf of the American Cancer Society, I am very pleased to be your host for this event. All the proceeds raised today will go to charity. We have some handsome guys and beautiful women for you to bid on. The top bidder will get to go on a dream date... and all it takes is a little bit of cash. So, don't be shy. Assisting me today will be the lovely Ashley Green. And, no fellas, she isn't for sale."

It seemed to me that this guy Mike definitely had a natural stage presence because he knew how to work the crowd.

Ashley was wearing an eye-catching red dress, "Hello everyone. Welcome! Are you all ready to begin?" She paused for reaction from the audience. "Come on, you can clap louder than that!" she encouraged the audience. They responded with cheers and applause. "Now, that's more like it!"

"Who is our first lady for sale?" Mike asked.

"Our first lady is Yvonne Channing," responded Ashley. "She is a Gemini, likes to play tennis, loves to travel, and is looking for a guy who is adventurous."

A pretty twenty-something year old woman walked up to the front of the room wearing a pink T-shirt and tight jeans.

"Don't be shy, Yvonne. Tell the guys why they should buy you," Ashley said encouragingly.

Looking rather bashful and as if she'd been put on the spot, Yvonne hesitated and then finally responded. "I have a good sense of humor."

"Anything else?" Ashley asked.

"Well..." Yvonne struggled to figure out what to add, "I've taken up cooking, so I can cook dinner for you if you buy a date with me!"

I leaned close to Tara and whispered in her ear, "She is cute, but she seems a bit timid and unsure of herself."

Tara looked at Yvonne and nodded. "You want to bid on her?" she asked.

Still close to her ear, I whispered again. "My money is spoken for. I can't bid on her and then on you, can I?"

Tara gave me a quick look. "You have a point. Maybe you should stick around to the end and try to talk to her."

Mike interjected, "A home cooked meal! Guys, you can't do better than that. Who wants to make an opening bid?" Surveying the crowd, Mike said, "Can I get 25 dollars? 25! Can I get 30? In the back, 30 yes! 40? Going for 40? Yes, 40! 50 dollars? 50? Yes, 50! 60? Anybody for 60? 60? Okay, 50 going once! Twice! Three times! Sold for 50!" Ashley walked over to the guy to collect the money and have him write down his information on a prepared card.

"We are off to a great start! Okay, now ladies, it's your turn to bid!" Mike said as Ashley returned to the front of the room.

"Yes, ladies, it's the moment you've been waiting for. This is Dom. He is an Aquarius; he is a film buff and likes to go hiking." Dressed in khaki pants and a polo golf shirt, Dom leaned into Ashley's microphone and said, "Hello ladies!"

"So, Dom, what would you like the ladies to know about you? What will a date with you be like?"

Ashley held her microphone in front of Dom as he thought of what to say. "Well, I am really into wine tasting and fine dining."

Mike turned to Ashley, "A night of fine food paired with the right wine and Dom. Sounds like fun, doesn't it Ashley?"

"It sure does. Do we have an opening bid?" Ashley asked the audience.

"Let's start at 25 dollars," Mike said to the audience. "Okay, 25 dollars, to the lady in blue sitting in the front."

I looked over at the lady in the blue. She looked like a classy, elegant lady. I'd bid on her if she were up for auction.

"Do we have 30?" The audience was silent. "Again do we have 30?" No hands were raised.

Ashley raised her hand, "I'm not sure if I can do this, but I'll take him for 30."

"Come on ladies! Are you going to let Ashley have him? How about 35? Do I hear 35?" Mike asked.

A guy in a gray T-shirt sitting with a bunch of his guy friends grinned and raised his hand, "Ok 35 to the gentleman in the gray T-shirt. Do we have 40? 40 anyone?" One of the guy's friends mockingly punched him in the arm and laughed as he raised his hand, "Alright, 40 to the gentleman in the green shirt sitting beside the man in gray," Mike announced.

Oh man, I felt bad for Dom. I'm sure it was all in good fun and maybe the guys were just trying to help drive up the bidding, but what if no one else bid on him?

"Well, this is an interesting turn of events! Hey, it's all in good fun and in the name of charity, but ladies, are you going to let Dom get away?" asked Ashley.

"That's right ladies, how about 45?" The woman in blue, who had made the initial bid, raised her hand. "Yes, 45 to the lady in the front wearing blue. Going once, going twice. Sold!" Mike exclaimed.

"Next, we have Sherry," Mike said as a tall woman dressed in flower-print summer dress walked up. "She is a huge movie buff, loves the theater, and has a soft spot for musicians."

"Guys, if any of you play any musical instruments, now you know the way to Sherry's heart," Ashley piped in. "So, Sherry, tell us, what can you say to convince the guys to bid on you?"

Ashley handed the microphone to Sherry, "Well... I can't really cook, but I can bake cookies. Yes, I will bake you cookies if you buy me."

The bidding went crazy. Sherry fetched 80 dollars. After Sherry, they auctioned off another guy, Gene. He did a little better than Dom. He looked pretty fit and he didn't seem like he was just some meathead. When he said he knew how to give Thai massages, it didn't sound like a cheap come on at all. In fact, it drove the bidding up. He received the highest bid of all the men that night, at 75 dollars.

Finally, they had saved the best for last. Okay, I am a little biased.

"Next, we have Tara Reynolds," Mike said to the crowd.

Tara smiled at me and walked up to the front. Good choice for the dress she picked. The deep purple color really suited her and it showed off her great legs.

"Tara loves art. She loves going to the Chelsea art gallery openings and dancing. Let's start the bidding at 25 dollars. 25 to the gentleman in black. 30, do I hear 35?"

Ashley interrupted Mike, "So, Tara, why should someone bid on you?"

"I can bake cookies, too, but I can give you something even sweeter for your lips," Tara said playing to the crowd. "I am a good kisser!"

Mike responded. "How lucky are you guys, a second woman who will bake you cookies! Cookies and kisses! Let's start at 40 dollars! Can I get 40?"

I raised my hand.

"Yes, we got 40! Can I get 50 dollars?"

A guy dressed in a green polo golf shirt raised his hand.

"How about 55?"

The man in black who had made the first bid raised his hand.

"Yes, 55! Tara, is there anything else you can add to why they should buy you?"

Tara flashed a mischievous smile and said, "I have a Playboy Bunny costume!"

Mike screamed, "Is it getting hot in here or is it just me?! Baked cookies and a Playboy Bunny costume! Can I get 60 dollars?"

A guy in a suit seated in the rear raised his hand. Tara seemed to enjoy the competition and I wondered how high I should bid for her to feel like she got a high-enough bid.

"60! Great! Can I get 70 dollars?" The suit again raised his hand. "70! Can I get 80 dollars? 80? Hell yes!" Mike raised his hand, "I don't know if I can do this, but I'll do 85." Mike seemed to have gotten caught up in the bidding war himself. "85 now. 90 anyone?"

I raised my hand, "100," I said.

"100 to the dapper gentleman sitting up here in the front." Again, he went to Tara. "Any last thing to say that would make someone bid on you?"

Tara put her right hand on her right hip and leaned to the left, "I will bake you cookies in my Playboy Bunny costume."

Mike was excited, "Guys! Cookies made and served to you by a Playboy Bunny! Can I get 110 dollars?" Gene, the fit guy who had gotten the highest bid of all the men on auction, raised his hand.

Back and forth it went between Gene and the suit, until the suit finally gave up. Gene was at 175 dollars. I raised my hand to outbid him. The final bid was 200 dollars. After Ashley came over to collect my donation and fill out some paperwork, Tara came over and gave me a kiss on the cheek and a big hug.

Postscript: By the way, she never did bake me cookies in a Playboy Bunny costume. I teased her about false advertising. She said she was a little pissed at me because she had wanted Gene to outbid me. How was I supposed to know that? If I were psychic, I could've made a lot of money in the stock market.

Warning Labels

(LUANA)

I was enjoying my freedom again now that I had finally decided to move on from Gianni. After Montoya befriended me at Juan's birthday party, I realized how obsessed I had been with Gianni and that I had been grasping at straws at the end of the relationship. Meeting Montoya had restored my faith in men. He showed me that there were a few decent men who weren't after just one thing.

I have always been very free spirited, but somehow I had forgotten all that after I got involved with Gianni. Looking back on it now, I realized that I had gotten totally hooked on him. We were incredibly compatible; both of us had high sex drives and we quickly became inseparable. Gianni would come and go as he pleased. Sometimes he came over to my place in the wee hours of the morning for a quickie before both of us went to work.

He was always surprising me by dropping by or asking to see me at odd times; it could be any time of the day. Sometimes, we secretly met in the middle of the day. That is what made our relationship so hot. It was unpredictable and consuming, but it also sometimes made it difficult for me to plan my social calendar.

Occasionally, when I was already out, he'd interrupt by calling or texting me, announcing that he wanted to see me and we would meet somewhere. I usually found a way to duck out of whatever I was doing or to get away from whomever I was with. I knew exactly what I'd be getting and I just couldn't get enough of him. There were steamy phone calls and suggestive text messages that heightened the anticipation leading up to our next rendezvous. I knew what I liked and wanted so when I found a man who met my needs, I was insatiable.

One thing that I had loved to do before Gianni was to go out clubbing alone. For me, it was completely liberating. When I went out on my own, I always knew very clearly if I was just out to have a good time by myself or if I was going to be open to the possibility of bringing someone home at the end of the night.

I enjoyed going to clubs alone. That's when I met some of the most interesting and beautiful people. There were dancers (exotic, modern, ballet, you name it), models, artists, and actors. One of the most memorable was a former gymnast/acrobat who performed nightly, hanging up high from the ceiling. There were also young, highly successful, independently wealthy men—the ones for whom success had come so early that they had never had a chance to play around in their twenties, and a decade or two later, they still didn't want to grow up. They were perfect to have a good time with. Of course, I often got propositioned and sometimes it was hard to refuse. But I knew what I was doing and if I was going to go home with someone at the end of the night. Most of the time, it was the man of the night who'd end up being the casualty. I was the one who wouldn't want to see him again unless he really impressed me.

Tonight I had met Bruce, a big, beefy bouncer who had been flirting with me all night. Gianni had been texting me all night and I'd been ignoring him.

"I'm going home now and you're coming with me," I told Bruce. "I know the owner. I fixed him up with one of my girlfriends a while back so I can get you out of your shift early." The cab ride home was a delicious blur. I couldn't tell what combination of fingers, lips, and tongue or other body parts he was using, but whatever it was that he was doing, it nearly sent me over the edge.

By the time we had gotten to my apartment, I realized that I had lost my panties and tried to maintain some sense of decorum as we walked past the doorman. But once we were in my apartment, we went at it again. I immediately unzipped him, uncovering his generous package and went to work returning all the favors he had done for me on the taxi ride home. Bruce stopped me and started kissing me with one arm around me. His other hand gently reached behind my ass and in between my legs, which he knew was already bare. I lifted my dress and we positioned ourselves toward each other. As he entered me, my phone started ringing, heightening the urgency of the moment.

"Keep going! Keep going!" I screamed not wanting Bruce to stop. Bruce continued thrusting and then I came but Bruce had not. After we stopped, I reached into my purse, which I had dropped nearby to look at my phone. Gianni had called.

"Babe never mind who called. Let's pick up where we left off," Bruce said.

"Yes, I think it's time to move things into the bedroom," I said to Bruce as I started removing my dress and walking toward my bedroom.

In the bedroom I got on top of Bruce, slid him inside of me, taking the driver's seat and started grinding him. Suddenly, we heard pounding on my door. It was Gianni demanding that I let him in. Fortunately, I had put the chain across the door just in case, as a precaution, when I had closed the door. All night Gianni had been sending me frantic text messages demanding to see me and asking where I was.

Gianni was now outside of my door yelling, "Luana, I know you're in there and you're not alone. Open the door!"

I stopped grinding all of a sudden as I heard the lock to the front door of my apartment turn and then the door smacking against the chain that restrained Gianni from entering my apartment. "Damn it! It's my ex. We broke up a few weeks ago and I know he's going to make a scene." I got off the bed and went to grab a robe.

"Hold on, don't do anything just yet," Bruce said to me as he got up to look for his boxers.

Gianni screamed, "Luana, you'd better let me in here or I'll continue yelling at the top of my lungs and I'll start talking about things that I know you wouldn't like me to share with your neighbors! I don't care who hears me or if someone calls the cops!"

I wouldn't put it past Gianni to do something like this. He was shameless. All the lies, the cheating, the deceit, it had all been too much for me. I had been in open relationships before, and they had worked, but they required complete honesty about *everything*, which Gianni was simply not capable of. If only we had really been in an open relationship, in which I knew where everything stood, then, maybe it could have worked and things would not have gotten to this twisted state. I lived life by my own rules, and had nothing to hide, but I didn't want Gianni yelling and disturbing all of my neighbors. So, I went to unchain the door and let him in.

"Gianni what is all this madness about?! I have someone here. It's over. You don't own me," I announced.

"Did you do this to me?!" Gianni demanded holding up his smart phone.

I looked at it and saw the website Montoya had recommended. I smiled knowingly.

"How dare you do this to me!" He pulled back his arm to punch me, but I squatted down to duck his punch. I'd learned this in my kickboxing class. 'Drop and duck' was a safe, unexpected move if someone was going to try to hit or choke you. Gianni's hand smashed straight into the wall making a dent.

Bruce had gotten his boxers on and now stood between Gianni and me. He shielded me and towered over Gianni who was now clutching the hand that had punctured the wall. Giving Gianni a stone-cold look, Bruce said, "Look, the lady has asked you to leave. I think you've done enough. Don't make me personally remove you."

I looked over at Gianni from behind Bruce and said, "Yes, I put all the details of what you've done and your photo on that website for all the world to see. I did it to warn all of the women you have messed with in the past and present… and the countless others that there could be in the future. I don't want you to hurt anyone else like you've hurt me."

"Luana this is ridiculous! You can't leave this up there. What if my business partners somehow get wind of this?!" Gianni protested.

"Well, that's not my fault, is it? You made your bed and now you must lie in it," I replied.

"Listen buddy, I think you've done enough harm tonight. Do I need to show you to the door?" Bruce said to Gianni.

"No, I'll show myself out," Gianni said as he walked toward the door and left.

"Sometimes I think that men like that should come with warning labels. That's why I decided to expose him on the Internet," I explained to Bruce.

"I think you know how to take care of yourself just fine," Bruce said.

"Well, I'm glad that you were here when Gianni showed up. I don't know how I really would have handled it if I were home alone," I looked at Bruce, took his hand and said, "Now, let me take care of you," and I led him back into the bedroom.

Boomerang Business Card

(TARA and Frank)

With the end of spring nearing and summer nearly upon us, it was perfect weather to be on a trendy rooftop bar in SoHo. As I stood by the bar waiting to order my drink, I noticed an attractive Asian guy already sitting there by himself. He wore a dark sports jacket and had a big, flashy gold ring on his hand that looked like it had some sort of a crest on it. After looking at him, I realized that I recognized him. While I never forgot a face, I was terrible with names. He looked over and smiled so I said, "Hi, I think we met earlier at the registration desk, I'm Tara. What was your name again?"

"Takao," he said as he extended his hand.

I shook his hand. "Oh, right, I checked you in. I meet so many people at these things it's hard to remember everyone's name. Every month I help out my friend Joanne at these happy hours." I liked feeling as though I were a part of the event. It allowed me to kind of play hostess for the night, and it made for easy conversational openings with people later on.

I waved at the bartender and said, "I'd like a lychee martini please. Thanks."

"So, what do you do besides organizing these events?"

"Oh, I'm just a volunteer. I help out with registration. I'm not the main organizer. My friend, Joanne Louie, is one of the organizers. I work in finance," I said my voice trailing off.

"Oh, you don't sound too enthusiastic about that."

"I guess it's just that I've been at my present job for a while now. What do you do?" I handed the bartender a twenty and took a sip of my lychee martini.

"I'm an accountant. Actually, I just moved back from California. Right now, I live up near Westchester and I'm really enjoying coming into the city for events like this."

"What part of California were you living in?"

"I was in L.A., but I grew up in Westchester. I have never lived in the city; so now I'm getting a chance to know it better."

"I see. Sorry, if you don't mind me saying, so, but I hate L.A.; the driving there is insane! I never realized this until I was out there a few years ago and rented a car to drive around. It takes about an hour to get anywhere and since I didn't know my way around, I got lost and ended up being an hour late wherever I went. I am so spoiled, I love New York and the convenience of it all."

"So, what do you do for fun in the city? Any suggestions?" Takao asked.

"Hmmm... besides the usual? Like going out with friends for dinner or to a bar or club? I really like doing new and different things. *Meetup.com* is a good way to find out about things to do. In fact, I started going to a *Meetup* group that goes to the art gallery openings in Chelsea on the first Thursday of the month. It's a great way to see new art and to meet people. We usually go for drinks or dinner afterward and that's when you really get to meet people."

"That sounds interesting. Maybe I should look them up."

"Yes check them out on *Meetup.com*. Do you have a business card or something? I could email you and invite you to join," I offered.

"Oh, I don't have a business card on me right now."

I put my martini down and reached into my purse, "Well, then, here's my card. You can email me and I'll put you in touch with them."

Just as I handed Takao my card, Rob came over and handed me a new freshly made lychee martini, "For you, my dear. Thanks for putting on another great event." As he said this, he put his arm around my shoulder.

"Thanks, Rob, I can always count on you for a drink or two! I'm not even done with my first drink. How have you been?"

"I'm great now that I see you here. I wouldn't miss this for the world. It's always such a good time!" Rob exclaimed. Rob was a former co-worker of mine who had become a good friend. I had the feeling that he was interested in me, but he was married and I never try to lead on married men. Maybe if he was single, I thought to myself.

And just like that, as so often happens, I got distracted and pulled into another conversation with Rob. Seeing this, Takao got up and walked to another part of the bar. I stepped away from the bar to scan the crowd as I continued speaking to Rob. With this beautiful weather, the rooftop bar was packed, and there were so many people to catch up with. I looked beyond Rob and saw Frank talking to a sexy brunette. Looking back at Rob, I remarked. "The turnout is really impressive tonight isn't it? Haven't seen you in quite some time. Where have you been?"

I felt a tap on my shoulder and turned to see one of the women I'd checked in at the registration desk earlier standing there with her hand stretched out holding a business card out to me. As I took the card from the woman who was dressed in a gray pantsuit, I heard her say, "Takao won't be needing this!" And she turned and walked away disappearing back into the crowd.

I stood there stunned as I looked at the card she gave me and realized that it was my own business card. Then, I remembered that Takao and the brunette had showed up at the registration desk at about the same time.

"What was that all about?" Rob asked.

"Can you believe it? Did you see that, a woman, the brunette wearing a gray pantsuit, just walked up to me and handed my own business card back to me, a business card that I had given to some guy earlier tonight. It happened so fast that at first I didn't realize what had happened. I'm speechless. I mean, who is she and how did she get my card from him, and what kind of guy would let a woman do that to him?! Talk about psycho," I said as I held out my own business card for Rob to see.

"Really?! That's nuts! Do you know her?"

"No, I think I just checked her in at the registration desk, but I was talking to the guy who she came in with, and I gave him my card as a friendly gesture. I certainly didn't mean anything by it."

"Whoa, I mean really?!"

"Yeah, even if she was his girlfriend or whatever, that is a bit much!" I said.

Just then, Frank walked up and handed me a cocktail napkin as he said, "The guy over there in the purple tie asked me to give this to you."

I saw that a phone number had been scribbled onto the napkin and looked over to see Takao, who winked at me. "Unbelievable!" I turned and walked into the crowd, tapped the shoulder of the woman in the gray pantsuit. As I dangled the cocktail napkin in front of the woman's face, I said, "I won't be needing this. You can keep it, and you can keep him." I turned and walked away feeling vindicated. I didn't want to have anything to do with Takao or his lady friend.

BOOK 1

SUMMER

From Russia with Sex

(LUANA, Montoya and Katia)

Montoya and I were sitting in the Roof Dining Room of the Yale Club, a clean modern space with high ceilings and grand arches. Across from us was one of my best friends, Katia Romanov, a svelte, bosomy brunette in her thirties. Katia always looked polished and put together. Her nails were flawlessly manicured just as her hair was always perfectly coiffed. The three of us were sharing a bottle of red wine and some appetizers.

"Gianni recently showed up at my door, late at night, but I had a big, muscular bouncer with me that night. I couldn't believe how desperately he was begging me to take him off the website you gave me," I told Montoya and Katia.

"So, that's how you finally got rid of him?" Katia asked in her Russian accent.

"Well, at first I put him on the website because I wanted other women to be forewarned about him, but after he showed up at my door, I took him off of the website because I could see why he didn't want people he worked with to see it," I explained. "And then, I told my doorman to never let Gianni into the building again. The doorman didn't know that we'd broken up. In the past Gianni was always coming over and so the last time Gianni showed up at my door, he just gave Gianni my spare key without even thinking about it. As I was talking to my doorman about what had happened with Gianni that night, we got into an interesting conversation about all the crazy things he's seen over the years."

"I'll bet!" said Montoya intrigued.

"What stories does he have?" asked Katia.

"He told me that there's this one woman in the building who always seems to come home at 4 A.M. on Saturdays, barely clothed and drunk. It's like clockwork, he says. She always looks like a wreck and her private parts are barely covered up! But on any other day of the week, she looks very prim and proper and behaves as if nothing of that sort ever happened!"

"Sounds like Dr. Jekyll and Ms. Hyde," Montoya said.

"Oh, and of course, there are always the crazy things people do in the elevator. One couple basically flashed the camera in the elevator before going at it. As a prank, the doorman rang the fire alarm to see if that would startle or stop them, but it seemed to have the opposite effect on them as they just went at it even more furiously!"

"Elevator sex, been there, done that," said Montoya.

"Yeah, and then there's this one annoying person who seems to always lose his keys and get locked out of his apartment. Oh, and even stranger, there's this person who once mistakenly came over to the building thinking he lived there, but it turns out he was at the wrong address. However, he still periodically comes over pissed drunk, claiming that he lives in the building."

"Always something interesting in the life of a doorman," Montoya added.

"Well, I gave the doorman some extra tip money and told him to make sure that Gianni was not allowed in the building again. I am finally, finally ending this bad, bad, bad relationship! Looking back on it now I realize that when I discovered that Gianni was bedding other women, sometimes on the same day as we had been together, I was furious. For a while, I felt entitled to do the same thing, which accounts for the sexual advances that I had made toward you and Frank the first night we all met," I said looking at Montoya. "I think

I was addicted to Gianni and the relationship that we had. But I am over it now. And it was all thanks to you. Thanks for talking some sense into me."

"You did a really good deed. God will bless you!" Katia said to Montoya.

"I am very glad I was able to help you," Montoya replied. "And Katia, I didn't think you were religious."

"I am similar to Luana. Not religious, but I am spiritual."

"I just did my part. Luana had to do the really hard part by setting boundaries with Gianni and sticking to them. People like Gianni will always test others' boundaries. But she is holding her ground," Montoya said.

"Now, Luana, you need to think about what kind of man you are looking for next," Katia said adamantly.

"Please, I just ended a relationship. I don't need to make any plans just yet. No relationships."

"What about you and Montoya?" Katia asked. "You seem to both get along great," Katia said looking back and forth at both of us.

"Our timing is off. I am on the rebound and I think he is too," I responded looking over at Montoya.

"Might I remind you ladies—I'm sitting right here. But, seriously, I went out on a date with someone recently and I found myself talking about my exes," he said taking a sip of his wine. "And, yes, I also realized that I am still a bit on the rebound, too."

"So, at the moment, I think we are meant to just be friends. I do feel that we are kindred spirits in a way and it would be good to have a real male friend to talk to and confide in," I said as I put my hand lightly on Montoya's.

"Of course, it will be hard to not think of you in a sexual way. You do realize that," Montoya responded.

"Well, this will be a first for me, and it may be hard to not think of you in a sexual way either," I said coyly as I leaned over to give Montoya a quick kiss on the lips.

"I'm not totally convinced about this friendship thing going on with the two of you," Katia said breaking the sexual tension between Montoya and me. Then she waved the waiter over to order another drink.

"So, what about you Katia? Any boyfriend?" Montoya asked changing the subject.

"Of course, you can't have a body like this and not have a boyfriend," Katia said laughing.

"Well, I am glad to see that you are humble as well as spiritual," Montoya jested.

"I always have a boyfriend and I am always the one doing the breaking up. Women these days don't get it. I think if I am having sex with a guy, he should be grateful. He should pay. Why should I be doing things for him and not get anything in return? It isn't fair. So, of course, my boyfriends have to pay my rent, buy me things, and take care of me."

"Sounds very materialistic. No?" Montoya responded.

"Not materialistic. No. I could have any guy I want. So, he should be grateful and do things for me. Why am I doing him and pleasuring him if he doesn't provide for me? That's not fair," Katia proclaimed.

"I love the Russian mentality. Very practical," I chimed in.

"American women. Why go to bed with someone and be used by these jerks? Get something out of it. Why is it so unfair? You're not going to see me feeling down about any guy. They may feel sad that they didn't treat me right and let me get away… look at what they are missing?" Katia boasted.

"What is your boyfriend like?" Montoya asked.

Katia laughed. "Dumb, very dumb. I don't mean stupid. He went to an Ivy League school and makes a lot of money as an investment banker."

"You mean he is dumb because he doesn't get it that you are subtly controlling him?" Montoya asked.

"See, you and I can never date. You get it." Katia laughed again. "I need a guy who I can train like a dog. Who'll roll over when I tell him to roll over, and control him but who doesn't realize that I am controlling him. Why do men become rock stars or CEOs? It is because then they can easily get a hot woman who is great in bed. Trust me! Behind every great man is an even greater woman!"

"I think Evita Peron would agree with you," I kidded.

"I need a guy I can handle. Make him do what I want, when I want and him never knowing who is pulling his strings." Katia took another swig of her drink, and then popped the cherry into her mouth.

"So, not *From Russia with Love*, but from Russia with sex?" Montoya said as Katia removed the cherry stem from her lips. She had managed to tie the stem into a knot with her tongue. Seeing this, Montoya and I both laughed.

Then, Montoya said, "With such a skilled tongue, it's no wonder you have men wrapped around your finger. So, are you planning on getting married to this current boyfriend?"

"Maybe. But I am always on the lookout for an even dumber and richer guy."

I listened to the exchange between Katia and Montoya, feeling amused.

"If all Russian women think the way you do, I'd be afraid to date them. I don't know if I want to eat milk bones and wear a dog collar for the rest of my life," Montoya joked.

"You don't know what you are missing. It is worth it." Katia said, swirling the drink in her hand.

Finding the Right Timing

(TARA and Roxanne)

Frank and I were having one of our regular Sunday brunches at the City Bakery when Roxanne Shapiro walked into our lives. I had gotten up to get some cutlery, leaving Frank sitting all by himself at the table. When I returned, there was Roxanne with her mass of curly blonde hair and matching bubbly personality, sitting in my seat chatting up Frank. However, I could tell that Frank was not interested in her. He doesn't usually like women who come on too strong, or are too forward.

Our Sunday brunch ritual started after I moved into my own apartment in Manhattan after getting my MBA from Columbia. I had met Frank when I was a teenager going through my awkward stage and still wearing braces. My first encounter with Frank was at my father's office. Frank had just started working at my father Nick's luxury car magazine. My father had taken an instant liking to Frank when he interviewed him. The fact that Frank was a fellow alum, having also graduated from Princeton didn't hurt either. He said that he saw something in Frank, so he took him under his wing.

For several years they worked together. Frank really knew cars, and loved them so much that he decided that he wanted to open up a luxury car dealership. Within a few years he had raised enough money from investors, including my father, to open his own luxury car dealership. With Frank's determination and charm it quickly became very successful. So he left the magazine and opened up a few more dealerships. Frank sometimes still works with my father on stories for the magazine, by providing vintage and exotic cars for photo shoots. My father now regards him as a peer. I had heard so much about Frank from my father.

When I was getting ready to move into my first Manhattan apartment, Frank offered to help me with the move. To thank him, I took him out to brunch. Frank and I had an instant rapport that first Sunday brunch. It was almost like we were family and Sunday brunches became a sort of regular ritual for us. I knew that my father would approve of our friendship and suspected that my father liked knowing that Frank was somehow keeping a watchful eye over me.

As I approached the table, Roxanne didn't miss a beat and I soon found myself looped into their conversation. Somehow, I couldn't quite figure out where I'd seen her before. Then, I realized that I had seen her on TV, reporting from the scene on some local news event. I immediately liked Roxanne's boldness and upbeat attitude. I would learn that she was direct, like Frank, who would always give it to me straight whenever our conversation turned to the subject of who I was dating.

Nothing ever happened between Frank and Roxanne. But Roxanne and I had exchanged numbers that day at The City Bakery and soon the two of us became close friends. We'd often go to events and mixers—just the two of us single girls. She was a member of the 92nd Street YMHA (the Jewish equivalent of the YMCA) and invited me along to some of their single events as her shiksa wing woman. She was funny, smart, and independent. Only a few years older than I was, she was in her mid-thirties, but she definitely looked much younger than her age.

She was one of those types of people who had no qualms about walking up to complete strangers and striking up conversations with them. Amazingly, she could chat people up on just about anything—trivial or controversial. I suppose that's what made her such a good television reporter. Her youthful attitude charmed people, and it was hard not to become engaged in conversation with her quick, friendly banter. She always seemed so genuinely excited to meet and talk to new people.

Roxanne told me that she had been engaged once. She had been with her fiancé, Cole, for eight years, when her life changed forever on the morning of September 11, 2001. He was on one of the top floors of Tower One for a meeting when it happened. She went into shock and disbelief when she learned this from his boss. As she mourned Cole's death, she took a leave of absence and became very socially withdrawn. It was hard for me to imagine her like that.

When a couple of weeks had passed, her informal mentor Donna Drake and several of her fellow co-workers, encouraged her to go back to reporting. Roxanne is one of the strongest, most resilient women I know. It is remarkable how optimistic she is considering what she went through. I've met her very friendly mentor Donna who is now hosting her own show called *Live It Up!* The show features stories of inspiration, hope and motivation, of which Roxanne is a prime example.

At events Roxanne never needed to have someone by her side and that's why we were such a good team. We would "divide and conquer." Since she knew how to talk to people, she was THE best wing woman! It also certainly didn't hurt that she was a local celebrity of sorts.

I'd heard about a screening of short films shot in Southeast Asia and invited Roxanne to join me. Growing up, I definitely went through various phases. As a child, I just wanted to fit in and be like the other kids at school. Then, in my teens, I wanted some definitive answers about my roots but hadn't been able to find anything out about my birth mother. So, I dropped it and stopped looking for answers in frustration. But recently I started to be curious about Southeast Asia and my roots again. As I thought about it, I appreciated how my parents had made an effort to share with me what they knew and had experienced of Thai and Cambodian culture.

Roxanne and I were at the movie screening after-party when she said to me, "Tara, he's looking over at you. Give me your business card." And before I knew it, Roxanne had handed my business card over to the man who had been looking at me. As Roxanne stood beside him, she waved me over. I had no time to be nervous and had no excuse to prevent me from going over to talk to one of the most handsome men I'd ever met. At more than six-feet tall, he was tall for an Asian guy. He was clearly in great shape and had the looks of a Hong Kong movie star.

"So, Tara, do you always have your agent here to do your bidding? Very impressive to say the least since you have a celebrity wing woman."

"Her talents are invaluable. You know my name already, what's yours?" I asked smiling.

"I'm Terence. Unlike you, I don't have any representation at the moment, but I hope that we can cut out the formalities and go-betweens. No offense to Roxanne here. After all, it's thanks to her that we've now been connected."

As we talked, I learned that Terence Liu was an aspiring filmmaker. He had been vacationing in Cambodia a year ago when he had come across the Nomi Network's efforts to eradicate sex trafficking in Cambodia and other parts of Asia. "Nomi" was the pseudonym of a young girl who had been a victim of child sexual exploitation. Now, he was making a short documentary about the Nomi Network.

I told him about my amateur experience behind the camera, which included experimenting with the making of a video log of my travels through Europe. After completing an MBA in Finance at Columbia, I had taken a month off to travel before starting my job search.

Initially, I'd planned to travel with a few friends, but one of them got a job offer, which required her to start immediately after graduation, and the other woman ended up going to Hawaii with her boyfriend who'd been pestering her to go away with him for a while. I was disappointed but happy for my friend who got her dream job and what about my other friend? It's a good thing that she decided to go to Hawaii because her boyfriend ended up proposing to her on the trip. I found a third person to travel with me, but when she canceled, I was left feeling a bit dejected and rejected.

Tired of having my travel plans derailed by others, I resolved to travel alone. My parents had given me a camcorder to document my trip. While traveling, I'd kept a short-lived blog of the trip under the alias, *Budding Europhile* so that my friends and family could follow along with me online. Every few days, I'd visit an Internet café and write a post for my blog. Along the way, I shot a few short video clips, and when I got home, I edited and assembled them into a video log of my trip. This stirred my appreciation of documentary films. The blog has been dormant for a few years now since I hadn't bothered to keep up with it once I'd returned from my trip. As we continued chatting, Terence shared some of the ideas that he had for documentaries that he'd like to shoot.

On the subway ride home, Roxanne declared, "I think he's going to call to ask you out to dinner."

When I got home, I checked my email and was surprised to discover Terrence had written me saying that he'd checked my blog about my European travels and that he'd continue to read more later. He must have remembered and googled my alias name, *Budding Europhile*. He wrote:

I am warning you ahead of time that I plan to ask you out. So, if you don't want that to happen, this is your chance to enter the witness protection program.

-Terence

I thought it was endearing, so I promptly wrote back:

Thanks for the heads up but I'm fine with you finding me, so here is my cell number.

Over the next few weeks, we exchanged a few light-hearted emails. A week and a half went by without any word from him and I started to wonder. Then, he emailed me that his wallet and phone had been stolen, along with his identity.

So, he couldn't call me as he had been dealing with this emergency. In the same email, he told me that he had replaced his phone. And he'd made reservations for us to have brunch on the coming Sunday at a restaurant that happened to be a block away from where I lived. He had remembered what neighborhood I lived in! Since he had emailed me about the brunch on Saturday, just the day before, I texted him back to confirm our date, thinking that that would be the most direct and immediate way to respond.

When I didn't hear back from him that night, I felt a bit uneasy. But the following morning, I went to the restaurant and waited, and then I waited some more. Thirty minutes passed. I wondered where he was. I left him a voicemail and also sent him a text asking what happened to him. He lived in the Bronx. Maybe there was a delay with the Manhattan-bound trains in the subway? Maybe he was running late? Finally, nearly an hour later, I left and walked home. I wasn't angry, just confused because he had been very consistent and direct about his intentions all along.

When I got home, one of my friends happened to call asking if I'd gotten any of his text messages. That's when it dawned on me, and I realized what had happened. There had been a HUGE miscommunication. My text message function was broken! Sure enough, I realized that I had not received any new text messages in the last twelve hours, and the ones I'd written probably hadn't been delivered.

I checked my email and sure enough there was an email from Terence sent that Sunday morning, written just a few hours before the brunch date. It read:

> From: Terence Liu
> To: Tara Reynolds
> Subject: Brunch
>
> ====================
> Are we still on for today? You haven't given me a green or red light.
> -T

I responded to his email explaining that I had answered him by text message, but he probably didn't receive it since my text messaging function was broken. I also told him that I had waited for him for an hour at the restaurant, and then asked if he still wanted to meet later that day. Not long after, he called.

"Hi, I'm sorry I can't meet now because I'm on call at the support desk today. I was supposed to work, but when we made plans to meet for brunch, I made arrangements to switch my shift with a co-worker. But then, when you didn't confirm, I decided to take the shift back so that my co-worker didn't have to work on the weekend for me."

I understood what had happened, but I was still disappointed. To top it all off, I was about to leave the country to attend a friend's wedding in Australia in two days. At this point, it all seemed a bit absurd, but it also seemed as though there was this unspoken obligation to still make the date happen.

So, we made another plan to meet on Monday for lunch near the office where he worked. It was the day before I was to fly to Australia. I'd planned a two-week vacation since I figured that after traveling all that way, I should take advantage of it. I'd arrive in Sydney a few days before the wedding, and tour around the city. Next, I'd be going on to the Great Barrier Reef for some scuba diving, and then I'd to fly off to Ayers Rock where I'd spend a few days trekking and camping in the outback, before returning to Sydney to fly back to New York.

I had a lot to take care of at work before leaving the next day, so I ended up arriving a little late for our lunch date. When I got there, he wasn't there. Trying not to feel too dissuaded, I promptly called him to let him know that I was at the restaurant. He picked up right away and said that he'd be right over.

Despite all these false starts, it was one of the most perfect first dates I've ever had. There was no awkwardness or superficiality; the conversation flowed easily. We just talked about ourselves, and the experiences that made us who we are today. He told me that he had always been a film buff and that it just seemed natural to study film in college. For him, films were a powerful form of storytelling.

Soon after graduating, his mother had gotten into a car accident, so he decided to move back to Taiwan to take care of her as she recovered. Afterward, he took the opportunity to travel around Southeast Asia. Upon returning to New York, he continued to work on a couple of film projects on the side. I found myself wishing that we had this wonderful date a few weeks earlier, not now when I'd be getting on a plane to go halfway around the world in less than twenty-four hours. I felt as if there was so much promise for this budding relationship.

However, I soon found myself in Australia. During my first few days there, I stayed with friends in Sydney and was able to IM and exchange a few emails with Terence. But it became difficult to stay in touch with him due to the time difference as I traveled around the country. I was in the outback and scuba diving so I didn't always have access to the Internet. Timing was not on our side.

When I got back, I tried to reach Terence. Not wanting to take any chances with text messaging or email, I called him but he didn't pick up so I left him a voicemail. It took him a few days to respond. Finally, he wrote me an email saying that he had accepted a job working for a new television channel in L.A. and was now living there. He suggested that we keep in touch on *Facebook*. But I realized that my moment with him had passed. Sometimes, relationships are a matter of timing, and sometimes, the timing is out of our hands.

The Jet-setter

(FRANK)

Blakely Turnbull was from one of the oldest and wealthiest families in New York. Her great-great-grandfather had started a small haberdashery in the mid-1800s that became a major national chain of department stores. The chain went belly up after it was sold to a competitor, but the family retained their great wealth by diversifying their investments into television and radio. Blakely was well known on the New York social circuit. I met her at the opening night of the Metropolitan Opera.

While I wasn't a fan of opera, each year I would attend to meet interesting people. I tried to stand out in the crowd amongst all the gentlemen in tuxedos, and it worked with Blakely. Blakely is fifteen years older than I am, but we had never dated. Yet she always flirted with me, and I was always obliging. Blakely, in turn, would invite me to many exclusive social events.

At a private party in her massive apartment on Park Avenue, Blakely introduced me to Misty.

"Misty, this is a man you just must know. Frank Branigan is the owner of several major car dealerships in the tri-state area. Watch out Misty, he is quite the ladies' man," Blakely said giving Misty a knowing look.

I looked over at the rather petite Misty who had blonde hair and a curvaceous figure. Suddenly, I realized who she was. Misty had gone triple platinum with her first album and was known for her provocative music videos. She was also known for her highly public love affairs in the ten years since she had become a household name.

"Pleasure to meet you, I really like your music videos," I said acknowledging my recognition of her.

"You are a very lucky man, Frank," Misty said as if to share her thoughts aloud.

"How is that?" I asked.

"I am in-between boyfriends and you just happen to be at the right place at the right time."

"How do you know if I am interested or available?" I said pretending to be indifferent.

"Yes, I heard about you. That you would play hard to get. Word on the party circuit is that you are great in bed."

"Who am I to disagree with the word of the party circuit?" I responded with a laugh.

I knew Misty would be in Manhattan for a few weeks before she was going to shoot another music video in L.A. So, I had to move quickly. On our first date, I took her to a Broadway musical. Outside of the theater the paparazzi were waiting for her. They immediately surrounded Misty and me. I was barraged by the endless sound of camera shutters clicking and flashes going off as they started snapping photos of her. Her bodyguards pushed the paparazzi back to clear the way for her to get into the awaiting limo. Misty dropped me off at my apartment, and gave me a long kiss good night.

"To be continued," I told her before exiting the limo.

The next day, Nine called to tell me that she had seen a photo of Misty and me in the tabloids. I took it in stride.

On the second date, Misty brought me up to her SoHo penthouse. Her personal chef prepared a meal for both of us. After the meal, she took my hand and led me to her bedroom. I unbuttoned her blouse and started lifting her skirt.

"So, let's see the package," she playfully demanded as she unzipped and dropped her skirt.

I undressed and Misty clapped her hands.

"Okay Frank, what do you intend to do to little ole me?"

"Take off your thong and you will find out," I playfully commanded.

I started French kissing Misty and slowly made my way down her body, licking her nipples and then her inner thighs. As I went down on her, Misty started moaning and panting until she had an orgasm. In return, Misty started to give me a blow job. Then, she reached into the drawer of her nightstand for a condom. I told her to turn around and we did it doggie style. This time, we climaxed together and collapsed on the bed. Afterwards, Misty reached into her nightstand again, took out a cigarette and lit it.

"I really am not a big fan of cigarette smoking," I told her.

"No problem, I only smoke one cigarette after a good lay. And that was a really good one."

"Well, I intend to give you many more good lays, so I guess I need to get used to that one cigarette a night," I quipped.

The next week while she was in Manhattan, I escorted her to a series of A-List only parties. I took my vintage Jaguar out of the garage so that I could personally drive Misty around in style. I had enough of her bodyguards. Finally, it came time for her to go to L.A. for a video shoot. While she was away, I called her daily. When the video shoot was over, I headed to the West coast to spend the weekend with her at her Malibu home. Unbeknownst to us, as we walked along the beach, the paparazzi took photos of us.

The following week, she had to attend a music awards event in London. After that, she headed to Paris for a charity function, and finally, she ended up in Milan for a fashion show. Every weekend,

I flew to each city to be with her. Altogether, I had left Manhattan for four weekends in a row to see her.

Over dinner in her SoHo penthouse, I thought it was time to discuss the subject of her tumultuous lifestyle. "Misty, you lead a whirlwind life and I am trying to keep up with you, but honestly I don't know if I can keep up with you for your upcoming tour. Also, I just want to punch the paparazzi who keep shoving cameras in my face."

"What do you want me to do? Slow down?" Misty asked somewhat defensively.

"Well, actually, yes. You've been a big success since you were eighteen. You have more money than most people can dream of. Why not slow up a bit?"

"Frank, you don't understand. I've been dreaming of this since I was a child star. I can't stop now. I am in my prime. You don't know the music business like I do. The public is fickle. If you drop out of sight for a while, the public goes for the newest fresh face."

"You are twenty-eight years old and I am forty-one. I am not as young as I used to be. I don't think I can chase after you on a world tour. Not unless I leave my business and become your personal escort," I said.

"Why not do that? I would love to have you on the road every day with me," Misty said enthusiastically.

"Don't get me wrong, you are great. But I need a certain amount of normalcy in my life," I responded realizing that my time with Misty was near an end.

"I'm sorry Frank. But right now, my career comes first," Misty said sadly.

Postscript: I saw Misty six months later when she was performing in concert at Madison Square Garden. She gave me backstage tickets and when I went backstage to see her, I also met her new boyfriend, a multimillionaire entrepreneur.

Always Wear Clean Undies

(NINE)

Jake Halliwell, a friend of Tara and Montoya, was more than six feet tall, blonde and attractive, but you wouldn't stop in your tracks for him. His personality was what made you take notice and boy, did this guy have personality. I found him to be rather self-absorbed but in a very charming and entertaining way. He'd talk and talk and talk, almost exclusively about himself. He was quite intriguing. His air of confidence probably came from his being a venture capitalist who had made a lot of money. He was the type to say something just to be provocative, but sometimes he was somewhat insightful. Our first conversation went something like this:

"So Nine, I can tell right off the bat that you are the type of girl who doesn't sleep around."

I smiled, "Really, how can you tell that? Maybe I am a total slut?"

"No. I know people and you are a waiter."

Still smiling, I said to him, "Sorry, buddy, I'm not a waitress. I am an attorney. Your insights are failing you."

"I meant—you wait for sex. You are the type who needs the guy to be hopelessly in love with you first before you sleep with him. Am I right? Come on, tell the truth," he said as if trying to get me to confess.

"Well, yes, I guess you could say that."

"But I also know that women like you who 'wait' are the best kissers. You burn with lust like a cat in heat and when you make out, it is with raw passion," he said as if he were impressed by his own words.

"If that is your way to get me to kiss you, I think you are playing the wrong game," I kidded back.

"No game, just total honesty. Now, I bet honesty isn't a game you are used to getting from men," he said obviously flirting with me.

This led to our first date, a movie. I was pleasantly surprised and amused that he could actually shut up for the length of the movie, though the movie was only an hour and a half long. On the way to dinner after the movie, he talked endlessly about what he thought of the movie and once again, it was hard to get a word in. I followed Jake as he walked in between two parallel-parked cars to cross the street, but I tripped and my knee gave out. I heard a pop. I fell to the ground and blacked out for a few moments.

When I regained consciousness, I felt a sharp pain in my leg and saw that I had popped my knee. As I looked up, I saw that a crowd had gathered around me and someone was calling 911. Jake, however, was not there. My skirt was hiked up to my boobies exposing the G-string I was wearing underneath for the entire world to see. I was lying on the side of my good leg. I couldn't see if my G- string was covering my privates, but from the way a teenage boy was gawking at me, I could tell they probably weren't private anymore. I was just glad no one had their cell phones out taking photos.

Jake, in the meantime, had been so wrapped up in his own commentary about the movie that he had walked one entire block before noticing that I wasn't walking beside him. Now, if that isn't self-absorbed, I don't know what is. Eventually, he noticed and backtracked to where I was. When he got there, he was shocked to see what had happened and said, "Nine are you alright?"

"Do I look alright? And where have you been?!" I yelled back at him.

"Step back, people!" he yelled, "There's nothing to see here," he said as he gently pulled my skirt down to cover my ass, and when the ambulance arrived, he went with me to the hospital. Of course, he talked nonstop on the way to the hospital.

I was in a knee brace and walked with crutches for three weeks. Jake wanted to go on a second date, but I told him no thanks. He was entertaining yes, but so focused on himself that he didn't realize that I, his date, was lying on the street with my privates exposed for the entire world to see. I was afraid that photos of me in a G-string would turn up on *Facebook*. Thank God, as far as I know, nothing has shown up. As my mother always told me—always wear clean undies, but in this case I'm not sure if it really matters when you're wearing a G-string.

Uninhibited

(TARA, Montoya, and Luana)

I admired the cluster of seashells in her hair. She was dressed in a bikini top and an aqua blue sequined fishtail skirt.

"Look, there's our first mermaid sighting of the day." Obviously, she was on her way to the Coney Island Mermaid Parade. "I must say that's a pretty impressive seashell hairpiece she has on," I said to Montoya and Luana.

"Indeed, I love how New Yorkers are so spirited and really get into it when it comes to their parades. And no one, except us, is even giving her a second look," Montoya commented.

"Yes, New Yorkers have seen it all. With all of the outlandish things that you see on the subway, New Yorkers have mastered this art of seeing something without acknowledging that they've actually seen it. On the outside, they have poker faces but I'm sure most people on this train have noticed the mermaid, but no one is even batting an eyelash. Nothing fazes New Yorkers," Luana added.

"I once saw this guy dressed as one of those green-plastic army soldiers riding the subway. He was completely green from head to toe: his face, his neck, and his hands were completely covered in green makeup. He was wearing green eye goggles and even had on these flat green pieces on the bottom of his boots to make him look like one of those plastic toy soldier figurines that stands on a plastic plate," I remarked to Montoya and Luana.

When we arrived at the Coney Island subway stop, the station was teeming with people. We saw a man who looked like he was covered in a dark green slime and had just broken free from a fishnet, the remnants of which were now stuck to him along with a starfish, a crab, and a few other fish. There was a woman in a blue wig. She was basically topless except for the seashell-shaped pasties that covered her nipples. Another woman wore a bunch of tropical flowers in her hair and not much else other than body paint. She had iridescent, green-blue scales painted over her boobs and parts of her torso. It was a totally carnival-like atmosphere.

At the parade some bead tossing occurred, but this crowd was much tamer than what you'd see at Mardi Gras in New Orleans. The costumes were definitely as impressive as what I've seen at the Halloween parade, except that they all had an aquatic theme. Plenty of people were dressed as sea creatures like jellyfish, octopuses, and fantastic mythical creatures with tentacles, tails, and scales. One of the most hilarious costumes was a guy dressed as an oversized lobster. Someone dressed as a cook was chasing him trying to get him into a pot of boiling hot water.

Montoya, Luana, and I had planned to hang out on the beach after the parade. I had prepared a picnic basket with sandwiches and munchies for the day. At the beach, Montoya happily helped Luana and me by rubbing our backs with sunscreen. After lying in the hot sun while trying to read, but dozing off a few times, I went into the water to cool off and Montoya joined me. Luana stayed on her blanket sunbathing.

Running from the waves as they crashed against us was fun. Each wave seemed stronger than the last. After getting my fill of this, I started to make my way back up to the beach when suddenly a wave hit me so hard that the back of my bikini top snapped open. Fortunately, it didn't completely fly off because it was tied around my neck and I caught the front of it in time.

"Are you heading back to the beach, love? Are the waves too much for you?" Montoya asked as he walked toward me. He apparently hadn't seen what had just happened.

"Uh, Montoya could you please turn the other way. Don't look over here. I need to adjust my bikini top." I had my arms crossed over my chest trying to cover up, "I'm just going to walk back into deeper water and try to put it back on."

"Are you sure you're okay? Do you need any help?" Montoya asked.

"Uh no, no, I'll be just fine," I was embarrassed and hoped that he hadn't seen anything.

"Tara, please. I don't want you to get knocked over by the waves. Let me help you. I promise I won't look," Montoya said as he walked over. "I'll stand right behind you where I can't see anything. Let me help you. I've certainly unfastened a few of those in my day, so I think I can figure out how to snap it back in place."

Montoya was standing behind me now. "Um ok," I said. Montoya reached over, took the two ends of my bikini and snapped them back into place. "Thanks," I said as I adjusted the front of my bikini.

We walked back up the beach in silence. We dried off and I offered him a sandwich that I'd made.

"Thanks for being such a gentleman Montoya."

"Sure, I'm always willing to help a damsel in distress," Montoya said taking the sandwich from me. "I'm here to help you protect your precious assets."

"Ha ha, very funny," I said.

"I didn't see anything. Of course, I'm a tad disappointed. But it's probably better that way," he said.

Luana heard our exchange and rolled over on her beach towel flashing her boobs at both Montoya and myself. She had unfastened the back of her bikini as she lay on her stomach sunning her back.

Now, bare breasted she sat up and said, "You do realize that in Rio everyone goes around practically topless on the beach. I have no problems showing off my precious assets. Besides, I really don't like tan lines."

"Hey, I didn't know there was going to be a show today at the beach," Montoya said. "But with all the practically topless women from the Mermaid Parade on the beach, you aren't the only one going topless today Luana."

On the trip back to the city, Montoya and Luana sat in a two-seater on the subway, and I sat in an adjacent seat perpendicular to them so that we could converse more easily on our way back to the city.

"So, from now on, I vow to protect your assets and whatever else you want to hide from the public," Montoya said to me.

"You don't want to protect my assets also?" Luana kidded.

"Well, I don't think you want to be protected," Montoya said responding to Luana.

"What are you trying to say? You think I'm a prude?" I asked.

"Actually, anyone seems like a prude in comparison to Luana. I have known other Brazilians and she is in a class all by herself," Montoya remarked. "Luana you should tell Tara about your rating system."

Luana began, "Let me first explain that I like to take the merchandise out for a test drive, if you know what I mean—before deciding whether to keep a man around. I developed a very simple rating system. You're rated a one, two, or three."

"You mean like three strikes and you're out?" I asked.

"No, it's more like one strike and you're out. If a man is rated a one, that means I've been with him once, and if he didn't already impress me, that's it. It's definitely not happening, so there's no second chance. I know what I like and how I like it," Luana said with a wink. "A one means that the sex was so horrendously bad or worse yet if the man's dick just doesn't do it for me by either length or girth, then there's nothing you can do about that. I'm not saying that bigger is necessarily better, but there is definitely a minimum requirement."

"So, how do you make it to two?" I asked intrigued.

"Well, if the first time was good, I'll sleep with the guy again, hence the two, just to make sure. But if it was not as good or better than the first time, that's strike two. I won't be wasting any more time, I'll move on," Luana explained.

Montoya and I exchanged looks. "I like what happens at three," Montoya said grinning.

"If a man makes it to two, and I am left wanting more, that's when I'll see if he moves on to a three. So, the third time, if he really seals the deal, I become insatiable. And I want him every day. I expect to be sleeping with any man that I consider my boyfriend on a daily basis. A three means that a man has fully passed the test and has my seal of approval. I think this is a great rating system and just think, if all women used it, I could just find out from a man's ex-lover if he was a one, two, or a three. It's good to know that a man's been vetted," Luana declared.

"Most women wouldn't appreciate it if a man revealed the criteria for his rating system but somehow when Luana explains her rating system, it comes off sounding feminist and empowering for women," Montoya commented.

"Somehow I think that you would have no problem if all the women on this train took off their bras and started burning them right now," Luana said in jest to Montoya.

"Every woman except the eighty-year old grandma over there," Montoya said laughing at Luana's suggestion.

Soon, we were back in Manhattan. I was the first to get off the train. Montoya and Luana continued on uptown. As I took a shower at home and washed off all the sand on my skin and out of my hair,

I thought about Luana's rating system. Who would've thought, given the circumstances under which we first met, that I'd be having a conversation with Luana about her sex preferences? So much for first impressions, but I have to admit, I've never met anyone as uninhibited as Luana. On the Richter scale of uninhibitedness, most people wouldn't rate me anywhere near Luana. But truth be told, I am far from being a prude. I just keep that side of me to myself.

Luana's one-two-three rating system wouldn't work for me. The first time is usually, well, so awkward, really awkward. Sure, the first time is exciting. There's curiosity, sexual tension, and a forbidden nature to it even. But after the deed is done, it doesn't always meet my expectations. I don't think that's because I have high expectations.

How could anyone expect to get it all right on the first time around—as it is with anything new that we try? And that's the point. I could probably count the number of good first times I've had, because, frankly, there weren't that many. It's not that I have any sexual hang-ups, but I just need to relax and it takes time for me and the man in question to find out what each of us likes. So, for me, it usually gets better over time, and with practice—that's the fun part of it, lots and lots of practice. Once I finally feel comfortable enough to tell or show a man what I want, when I'm able to completely let go, then things really start falling into place.

I don't understand why women have one-night stands, unless they really know what they want and how to get off. How could someone be that uninhibited the first time around? Not everyone is as free as Luana. How can a woman be satisfied by a man who doesn't know exactly what she likes or what would get her off?

Beyond the thrilling, naughtiness of having sex with a complete stranger, someone new, unknown, and different, what is the point if the sex just isn't all that great and if you'll probably never see that man again? Where one-night stands are concerned, I'd rather have a vibrator. At least that way, I'd know that my needs would be met.

You could hardly say that I have been aloof with my lovers. I have always been very demonstrative and affectionate and have no problems with PDA—public displays of affection. In fact, when I was younger, I didn't seem to care at all about PDA. Once I nearly got caught for indecent exposure near the Lincoln Center Fountain. Had the cops arrived five minutes earlier, maybe I would have gotten arrested by the police for engaging in public sex acts, but by the time they arrived on the scene, it was too late; there was no "hard" evidence left.

I've never really cared what complete strangers might see or what they might be thinking when I'm out with my man. But when I'm out with friends, especially if some of them are not paired up, I do realize how this might offend their sensibilities, so I'd be a little more discrete. But whenever I'm out without a care in the world, and it's just my man and me, I do as I please.

Actually, I have come to realize that I kind of like public displays, or semi-public displays. There's something deliciously naughty about them, like the time I was standing on the sidewalk of First Avenue and I whispered into my date's ear, "Can you tell what I'm wearing underneath this?" He took it as an invitation to slip his hand underneath my wrap dress to find out that I was wearing a skimpy G-string. He kept his hand up there as he discretely hailed a cab with his free hand. He kept his hand there during the cab ride home, and it drove me nuts. By the time we got back to my place, my panties were off, and he used his hands in even more creative ways.

Maybe there's something of a closet-exhibitionist in me. Once I did it in the bathroom of a lounge bar. My man at the time had followed me in there, and one thing led to another. When we exited the restroom, and walked back to our table, people clapped and whistled.

Another time, my current boyfriend and I were staying in the living room of his sister's one-bedroom apartment. In the middle of the night, we went into the bathroom, outside of his sister's bedroom. Both of us faced the wall-to-wall mirror, and he entered me from behind. I could barely contain myself to stop from screaming, but my boyfriend wasn't as discreet, so I turned around and put my hand over his mouth. Then, I positioned myself on the counter facing him with my legs spread open and ready to receive him.

Another time, I was invited by one of my former lovers up to the roof of his building, and when he lifted my dress, I slipped out of my panties and didn't care who could hear us or see us. I didn't care if the people in the building across the way had a clear view of us. In the heat of the moment, who cares about things like that?

Oh, and another thing, I don't have any hang ups about blow jobs. In fact, I enjoy giving them. That's because I know how to give them and I like to think I'm pretty good at giving them, too. It's definitely made things a lot more interesting and enjoyable for the men I've been with. And yes, I've done them at unpredictable times and in unpredictable situations. The women who don't give blow jobs—it's probably because they have never learned how to do them successfully. So, it's no wonder that it ends up being a chore for them.

I bet you'd be surprised at the things people have done when it comes to sex. They just won't admit to it. I wonder what dirty little secrets people have about what gets them off.

The Exception

(Montoya)

I stepped out of the elevator with eight women friends of mine who I'd invited along to an 85 Broads mixer. The enclosed rooftop bar was wall-to-wall women. Some looked fresh out of college and some looked like seasoned professionals. All of them looked sharp and businesslike. I immediately spotted my friend Krista Sande-Kerback, a pretty blonde who went to Dartmouth and then to Columbia University for an MBA. She was the former head of strategy for 85 Broads, which I've always viewed as the best women's business networking organization in New York.

What was I doing here? Krista had told me that the organization was not exclusive to women—there was an exception to the women-only rule. Men could also join under the Guys That Rock program; so, I joined. Now, whenever I am at an 85 Broads mixer and women ask me what I'm doing there, I tell them the truth; I am a bona-fide member.

This time, I had brought eight women friends with me to introduce them to the organization. I thought that they might be interested in joining themselves. And, I did invite one other man, my mate, Jack Li, an ambitious, charming young stock trader. Since he always had an eye out for new business contacts, I knew that this would be a good networking opportunity for him. I planned to introduce him to Krista, who could tell him how he could become a member.

Five years ago, I was at an 85 Broads event when I met Tara. That time, I had arrived with only five of my women friends, and

Tara was curious about me, the lone guy surrounded by women. We hit it off right away. Through her I met Frank, and he and I instantly became wingmen for each other. We became close friends and partners in the pursuit of women.

My philosophy of meeting women is simple. When most men find out a woman has a boyfriend or a husband, they move on, but not me. My basic premise is that pretty women have pretty friends. Who cares if they have a boyfriend or a spouse? If I make friends with a pretty woman who has a husband or boyfriend, I figure, I am making friends with all of her friends as well. So, when they have a birthday party or some other event, I will meet this married woman's pretty, single women friends. Attractive women, even if attached, probably have attractive, single women friends. This plan seems so simple to me, but to other guys, it was like trying to untie the proverbial Gordian Knot. At every mixer or party, I just try to connect with at least one attractive woman.

Do that once a week for a year, and you will have fifty attractive women in your life. At the end of a few years, you will be meeting more attractive women than you know what to do with. In the past couple of years, I have added so many women to my *Facebook* list of friends that I can honestly say that I know a Dixie, Trixie, Sally, Halle, Bella, Ella, Staci, Tracey, and let's not forget April, May, and June or Honey, Candy, and Sugar. I even have Mi, Yu, and Hu on *We Chat*, China's version of *Facebook*.

One of the women I had invited tonight was my friend, Constance. Constance is a case in point for making friends with a beautiful woman who has a boyfriend or a husband. Constance is a Brit who married Omar, a member of a rich Lebanese-Christian family. She recommended me for membership at Frederick's nightclub, which was right next to the Paris Theater on 58th Street near Fifth Avenue. It is now closed but was a happening place to be in its day.

The front section was open to the public but the back area was a members-only section.

Many of the members were celebrities. Soon after getting accepted into Frederick's on Constance's recommendation, I got an invitation for a private reception at the club to meet a celebrity who had been a centerfold. She was to be there in the company of several "bunnies." How could I have passed that up? So, I invited several mates to come also, including Frank. At the party Frank and I made some new friends, and soon thereafter we were invited to a party at the West Coast mansion. My point is that none of this would have happened if I hadn't made friends with a beautiful married woman.

Constance, who was dressed in a pinstripe, navy blue business suit, spotted me talking to Krista and Jack. I motioned for her to come and join us.

"So what do you say we move on to the next event?" Constance asked Jack, Krista and me. She had invited us to an exclusive party on Fifth Avenue in a very posh hotel.

"Sounds good. What do you think Jack?"

"Let's do it," Jack said. "Krista, are you in?"

"I still need to talk to a few other people tonight, but the three of you go ahead and enjoy yourselves," Krista said.

Constance had also invited the women I brought to the 85 Broads event, so the plan was for all of us to do both events and to eventually meet up at the hotel party at the end of the night. So, Constance, Jack, and I went ahead first and jumped into a cab.

At the party, I recognized many celebrities. Jack noticed that a statuesque woman was keenly watching me.

"I think you have an admirer," Jack said. "She looks really hot but she looks older than you."

"I usually don't date older women. However, I do one day plan on being a dirty old man," I joked.

"That is bad," Jack replied.

"That's what they tell me. But I also heard that women like bad boys," I said making a wisecrack.

I walked over to meet her. She looked to be in her mid-forties but was still a real looker with great legs, dyed blonde hair, and what appeared to be a very well done boob job.

"Hi there, I'm Montoya. You look like you were either a Miss America contestant, a model or maybe even a centerfold. Am I right?"

She threw her head back with a laugh, and then took a sip of her drink. "I am Vonnie. And yes, you are right, you could say that I once had a staple through my navel in one of *those men's* magazines back in the early nineties. Is it that apparent?"

"Well, my dear, you are drop-dead gorgeous and have the confidence of someone who is used to causing car accidents as you walk down the street."

It had been more than twenty years since her centerfold days. Vonnie was now a successful, respected businesswoman and an independent film producer. She had been involved in several big Hollywood projects. I told her that for years I had been working on writing screenplays and had taken classes on producing at The New School. I ended up shagging her that night and she was so good that I immediately forgot about the age difference.

By the way, it was a very, very good boob job and she had an energy level in the bedroom equal to a woman in her twenties. We lasted for a month together. It ended when she went back to her former boyfriend who was ten years younger than I was. She told me that we would stay good friends and promised that she would read any script that I would write. She assured me that she would connect me to several big shots in Hollywood whenever I was ready to make my move from lawyer to screenwriter/ producer. Success to me really is all about networking and developing contacts.

I guess I misled my friend Jack about not dating older women because this amazingly hot MILF was someone I really wanted to connect with, and just like the Guy That Rocks program, there is always an exception to any rule.

Postscript: With members in more than one hundred different countries, 85 Broads was purchased in 2013 and renamed Ellevate. Jack Li moved back to China and got engaged, and Krista Sande-Kerback married a nice Taiwanese investment advisor here in New York City. Congratulations to the happy couples.

Three-Sided Odyssey

(NINE)

Nine was getting ready for what she thought was a first date, well she hoped it was, but then again, she wasn't quite sure if it was. She had known Andrew for about a year and they had a lot of friends in common. So it was hard to tell what exactly was going on.

Nine's Story:

One of my good friends, Quinn, had gone to school with Andrew, so I knew that he was a good guy. I sometimes saw him at church and periodically at some mutual friend's birthday party. He had a really great smile and the suave looks of a Bollywood leading man. We definitely had some sort of mutual attraction between us. Andrew and I used to talk about food and compare opinions on which places we thought had THE best burger, THE best pizza, THE best cupcakes, THE best sushi, THE best you name it.

But I had been too wrapped up with Paul to think of him *that* way. Months after I realized that it was finally over with Paul at Juan's birthday party, Andrew and I were talking about this new restaurant opening that we'd both heard about from our foodie friend, Cindy Zhou. Andrew mentioned that we should go there together some time. For a few weeks afterward, we exchanged short emails back and forth trying to find a time that worked for both of us. So, when the time came I wasn't even sure it was a date, but I hoped it was, or that it would lead to a real date soon.

When the day arrived he said he'd come by my apartment to pick me up. He arrived a bit early and I was still getting ready. At the time, my friend Kate from Ohio was staying with me while she looked for a job and a place of her own. So, she answered the door for me and talked with Andrew as he waited for me in the living room. They had met before. Since Kate was new to New York, I had invited her along to a few of my friends' birthday parties and social events.

After completing a few finishing touches with my makeup and putting on my earrings, I was ready. I walked into the living room and saw that Kate had changed out of her jeans into a dress. She looked like she had plans to go out somewhere, and then she said, "Andrew was telling me all about Odyssey. I've been wanting to go. Did you know that Patrick, who's in culinary school is a sous chef in the kitchen there? I just called him up and he said he'd take good care of us tonight."

That was it. Kate had somehow invited herself along on what I thought was supposed to be a date. Was she really that clueless about what was going on here? And why didn't Andrew put his foot down and say that he had already made reservations just for the two of us? I didn't know what to say. Did he invite her along himself or was it because she had called Patrick? So, the three of us went out. It was odd; during the dinner I was looking for clues that Kate was hitting on Andrew, but I didn't see any. At least, it was a great dining experience, and Andrew didn't flinch at all when the bill came and he announced that the entire dinner would be on him.

But Andrew and I, we never did make any other arrangements to actually go on a "date" after that and I was left wondering.

Andrew's Story:

I was really interested in Nine and glad to hear that she had finally moved on from this guy, Paul. I'd always thought she was so smart and sweet. We definitely had this really easy rapport. She was a real foodie. We had that in common. And when I saw the opportunity, I asked her out to dinner when the highly anticipated new restaurant, Odyssey, opened. I was definitely interested and had wanted to get her out on a date. When I arrived, her friend Kate answered the door since Nine was still getting ready, so I talked with Kate as I waited for Nine.

"Nine mentioned that you were coming by. So where are we going tonight?" Kate had asked.

"To Odyssey, which just opened last month," I said, wondering why she had said "we."

"Oh, right, Nine has been wanting to go. Our mutual friend, Patrick, who's in culinary school is actually doing an externship there. Let me call him up and see if he can hook us up for tonight. The reservation is under your name right?" Kate asked as she picked up her cell phone and started dialing.

Before I could even say anything, Kate was talking to someone on the phone and had hung up.

"Patrick said that he'd make sure that we get some real special treatment. I'm so excited about this!" squealed Kate. "Let me go put something else on and grab my purse!"

I wondered if maybe there had been some sort of miscommunication or misunderstanding on my part. Maybe Nine had invited her along. She was always inviting Kate along to things. Maybe this was her way of keeping things casual? Besides, Kate seemed so excited to go, and she had gotten us an upgrade. I just didn't have the heart to tell her that she wasn't invited along. Nine didn't seem to mind, and since I'd planned to treat Nine, I just decided that the entire dinner would be on me.

Kate's Story:

I think that Nine and Andrew are lucky that they got some special treatment tonight because I called up my friend Patrick. I think they should be thanking me right about now.

Postscript:

Nine: I wondered if Andrew might have been interested in Kate or maybe I had been mistaken and it wasn't a date at all. Andrew and Kate never seemed to develop any sort of individual friendship, let alone go on a date. Andrew and I fell back into the old pattern of a friendship at a distance—bumping into each other periodically over the next couple of months at the gatherings of mutual friends.

Andrew: After this, Nine seemed kind of distant and uninterested, so I just let things be.

Kate: I think it's about time for me to finally move out of here and find my own place. Nothing against Nine, but she is cramping my style.

The Open Door Policy

(LUANA)

One of my exes gave me the nickname of "Luanatic." It was a play on the word lunatic. He said I was crazed for sex. But I disagree. When it comes to dating, I have an open door policy. I simply like having variety and trying new things. As long as I know it won't kill me, why not give it a shot? To me, variety is the spice of life.

Also, I don't care what color you are. I'll mack with black; I'm down with brown; I'm mellow with yellow; and I'm all right with white. I'll give most men a shot, especially if I'm in the mood, tipsy, or horny enough that night. But most importantly, it depends on whether I am attracted to something about you—be it your smile, your laugh, your eyes, your personality, your intelligence, your looks, or simply that big bulge in your pants. Also, I'm not one of those people who'll regret my past explorations. To me, all my past experiences have made me the woman I am now.

I've been with all shapes and sizes. There was this fat guy. He wore horn-rimmed glasses and had a zany sense of humor. I told him he needed to get into shape and he responded back that he didn't consider himself out of shape. He said that he was round and that round was a shape, wasn't it? Come to think of it, I've heard that line before. Don't we all have a cousin who's said that? Funny guy, the fat guy, but I only had sex with him one time because I was worried I would give him a heart attack.

On the other spectrum of things, there was an eighteen-year-old who was very energetic, and eager, but he came too quickly. When that happened, I actually considered teaching the boy a thing or two, not just for my own benefit, but also for his future lovers.

My first time in a threesome happened in the closet of a club in the East Village. I was kind of drunk and I took this guy and his friend into the closet there. Let's just say that I made sure that they were satisfied and then they were more than ready to return the favor to me a few times over. I guess it's true what they say; it's good to give before you receive. My gay girlfriend, Sheryl, had always wanted me to become bi, but instead of coming out of the closet, I ended up going into one—with two guys no less.

Finding men isn't very hard at all. If you're available, they're available. Trust me, even if you are very overweight or unattractive; there is a man out there who wants to have sex with you. The problem is just weeding out the married ones who are lying about their marital status. I sometimes like to frequent the Meatpacking District. It's quite a people-watching scene. It is the place to see and be seen. There, you'll find a bunch of young things in tight little dresses shivering in the cold because they refuse to wear coats in the winter.

I'm proud to say that my tits can still compete with the best of them. In the summer I sometimes don't wear a bra, which is especially effective when I'm waiting in line to get into some hot club. As soon as the bouncer would see my two beautiful nipples, the door would open for me every time. And then, there are the cougars out on the prowl. Someone, pulzee tell the cougars, especially those who've gone on to being prehistoric saber tooth tigers, it's time to retire. I say that now, but I wonder how I will be when I have gotten to their age.

When it comes to meeting men, some women like mixers and parties, and I'm okay with some of that. Some go for speed dating but that really isn't my cup of cappuccino. Others like birthday parties since it's a great way to meet friends of friends. That way, you can rest assured your friends have already vetted the guy. As matter of fact, I love it when a friend of mine has already slept with the guy and I can get a review or rating of him. Why waste time with losers and guys who are bad in bed? A woman needs a screening process.

But I think that the opportunities to meet someone are all around us—whether it's waiting in the checkout line of a grocery store, walking your dog in the park, or maybe chatting with your next-door neighbor. You don't have to be like me, But if you're open to it, you'll see that there are more opportunities around than you think.

Metropolicks

(MONTOYA)

One of the myths about Asian women is that they are submissive. While I don't know how it works between men and women in Asia, I think this myth is absolutely not true. At the age of twenty-six, I fell in love with Mai. She was Vietnamese, the same age as me, and a phenomenon in bed—definitely a force of nature to be reckoned with. Mai was free spirited, fun, and energetic. She was fiercely independent and already had two children from a previous marriage.

We met in London when I was in the joint law degree program between Harvard Law School and Cambridge University. Our relationship was pretty serious. In fact, I had met her two children and they liked me. After graduating, my heart was set on moving to New York City and I went as planned. But Mai's entire support network was in London—her parents, her friends, and her kids' friends. Long distance relationships have never worked for me. I actually have no stomach for it. A long distance relationship gives neither party any happiness. There's just too much longing and no satisfaction. It results in what I call the "five-finger blues"—in other words, satisfying your needs yourself so as not to cheat with someone else. Unfortunately, Mai basically gave me an ultimatum saying that if we were to have a future together, it would have to be in London. I know this may be hard to believe, but if Mai and her kids had moved with me to New York City, I would probably be married right now.

Most of the women, who come from all corners of the globe to make the Big Apple their home, are among the most competitive, independent, aggressive, and ambitious women in the world. It's either that, or they will have to soon learn how to survive in this big city. I thought that Mai would have had no problem adjusting to life in New York. However, it was not to be. Yet, Mai and I have stayed in touch and I see her, her kids, and her new husband whenever I visit my parents in London.

About a month ago, I was at my friend Piper's birthday party for her five-year old son. It was held in a section of the Boat Basin in Central Park. Piper had hired a clown to shape balloons into animals and other objects for the kids. She also arranged for an ice cream bar with every topping imaginable where you could make an elaborate ice cream sundae concoction, or just get a plain old scoop of ice cream.

As I approached the ice cream bar, I noticed a stunning Asian woman. She was dressed simply in a white tube top and very short shorts, which showed off her slender figure. Her long, dark hair fell off the side of her long neck as she licked ice cream off an ice cream cone. The ice cream was quickly becoming liquefied in the summer heat. "You really need to lick it before it melts," I said as I approached her from the side with some napkins in my hand, I saw that what she was having actually looked more like sorbet. The way that she was dressed, she looked like she belonged in a sexy K-Pop video.

"Thanks for coming to my rescue," she said taking the napkins from me. "I'm trying not to make a mess here, especially since I'm wearing white," she paused. Then, seeing that I didn't have an ice cream cone she asked, "So where's your ice cream?"

"I was going to check out all the options at the ice cream bar, but then, I saw you and your little meltdown situation happening. I think that even with these napkins you need to act fast before there are any fatalities."

"I don't think there's time," she said struggling over the cone, which was now dripping. "I'm going to have to go in for a bite," she said with a suggestive smile and leaned in toward her ice cream cone.

"I'd like to know what flavor that is considering the way you are devouring it. That actually looks like sorbet, not ice cream."

"Yes it is a combination of mango and raspberry sorbet, but I actually wanted to get a scoop of green tea ice cream. Unfortunately they don't have any. Have you decided what flavor you're going to have at the bar?" she asked motioning to the ice cream bar.

"That's too bad because I like green tea ice cream too, but now I think I'm going to have to get the same as you. Yours looks so good."

"I'm Soo-Jin. What's your name?" she asked as we walked over to the bar.

"My friends call me Montoya," I said. "Could you give me a bit of the mango sorbet and the raspberry sorbet together in a cup?" I said to the server. As he handed me the cup with a spoon, I turned to Soo-Jin and said, "This way it won't melt so fast."

"So Montoya, where are you from? I hear a British accent but Montoya doesn't sound like an English name."

"I was raised in London but I'm half-Spanish and half-British."

"So, do you consider yourself white or Hispanic?"

"Actually, both."

"Obviously, I can hear your British accent, but I'm wondering if you can also speak Spanish?"

"*Sí, por supuesto,*" I responded.

"So, I take it that means yes, you do speak Spanish," Soo-Jin said.

"And what about you, Soo-Jin, that sounds like that might be a Korean name."

"That's a good guess. You must have a lot of Asian friends to know that."

"Yes, I do know many Asians. As a matter of fact, I met Piper at a Lunar New Year's party, hosted by the group Asian in New York."

"Sounds like an interesting group and event, I'm going to have to look them up," Soo-Jin said.

"Yes, you can look up their website or find them on *Facebook*, of course. They run a lot of great events throughout the year. What's interesting about the Lunar New Year party is that I learned that although a lot of people refer to it as the 'Chinese New Year,' many other Asian countries celebrate this holiday, hence the term, 'Lunar New Year.' I believe the Lunar New Year is celebrated by Koreans, right?"

"I grew up on Long Island and I know that more and more Korean Americans are celebrating it these days, but I'm not so sure that people in Korea do. It's nice to meet a non-Asian guy like you who seems genuinely interested in Asian culture. Last night I was out with some friends when a Caucasian guy tried to pick me up by asking if I was allowed to date outside of my race. When he said that, I just cracked up."

"If he hadn't blown it with that line, would he have been your type?"

"I haven't actually dated any Caucasian guys, not that I'm not open to it. I'm curious, although I think that my parents are traditional. They'd like me to end up with a Korean man."

She agreed to go out with me and our first date was to a little candlelight tapas place where I found out that her long neck was indeed tasty as we made out in the corner table of the restaurant. A few dates later, she invited me up to her apartment, which led to a make out session on her couch.

As we made out, Soo-Jin reached her hand down to unbutton my pants. Soon she was unzipping me and as she moved down, she said, "I think it's time to figure out what flavor you are." Then she started lightly licking my shaft up and down and then started using a combination of her hand and mouth together. Her motions became faster until she brought me to orgasm.

A few moments later, I started to remove her clothes and discovered that she was wearing red, see-through panties, which I removed. Then, I started to go down on her. She started to moan as I spread her legs further apart to give me room to use my fingers. I began stroking her in a come-hither movement while I continued licking her. After her first orgasm, I didn't stop and continued until she had her second orgasm. At that point, I raised my head to see if she still wanted more. "Don't stop," she said. So, I continued and after the third time she climaxed, she was spent and ready to fall asleep.

I felt like Soo-Jin and I were becoming an item, so I brought her with me to my friend Lucy's dinner party. Lucy hosted these quarterly dinner parties in her gorgeous loft apartment near Central Park. The parties were always quite impressive since she was a master of food preparation and presentation. Usually she invited eight people—four couples. Since Soo-Jin didn't drink, I warned her that most of the beverages that Lucy served at her dinners would be alcoholic. So, she brought a bottle of green tea to have something else to drink and to share with the others. I brought a nice bottle of port.

When the evening arrived, Soo-Jin and I were running late so I called Lucy to let her know and told her to please get started without us. When we arrived, everyone was already seated at the table, which was full of several platters of food. Each dish looked like a miniature piece of art. I immediately joined the table and Soo-Jin sat beside me, hastily putting her green tea on the floor. Soo-Jin tried to participate in the dinner conversation but was a bit preoccupied because she had to respond to emails from work on her phone.

She was a financial analyst covering the Korean and Japanese markets and trading had started since it was already the next day over there. In between emails, an unexpected development came up requiring her input and attention. Finally, she excused herself to make a phone call in the living room and then returned to join everyone for dinner.

The next day, Lucy called me to tell me that the other couples had complained afterwards that Soo-Jin hadn't shared her green tea.

"Are you serious?!" I said raising my voice unintentionally but then realizing this, I lowered it to try to reason with her, "Lucy, there wasn't any room on the table for the green tea when we got there and no one asked her for it."

"The other couples also thought that Soo-Jin was rude for texting at the table," Lucy complained.

"She was answering emails for work and who are these arses anyway to question what she is doing at the table? Why weren't they friendlier to her?" I said feeling annoyed about the whole situation.

Needless to say, Lucy didn't see my point of view and I was banned from her dinner parties. I never did tell Soo-Jin about the Lucy situation. Besides, my relationship with Soo-Jin came to an end soon after all this, when Soo-Jin told me that her family was going to introduce her to a Korean man. I will always remember how great Soo-Jin was in bed. I guess I am still looking for someone like Mai, only this time on the same continent.

In the dating pool of New York City, people can and do like to experiment. You could say that dating is like sampling a variety of flavors in an ice cream shop before choosing one. Or for those who can't decide, you could always get a double or triple scoop, depending on whether you're willing to do the extra licking. The choices can seem endless in this *Metropolicks* that we call New York City. Some like vanilla, some prefer chocolate, and some, like me, like green tea ice cream—but don't worry—there's enough ice cream for everyone.

BOOK 1

FALL

Sometimes You Have to Lie

(TARA)

One day you feel it—a change in the air—and you realize that the humidity of New York summers has gone, vanished into thin air. And then, you're left wondering how is it possible that the year is already more than half over? Whether or not you're ready for it, the signs are everywhere. Clothing displays in the stores have gone from summer dresses and strappy sandals to long-sleeved items in dark earthy tones. Winter will soon be upon us. Some might find it depressing, but I was excited. Although it was practically fall in New York, for one week spring would be coming to town—Spring/Summer Fashion Week that is!

Fashion Week is the ultimate New York insider's event. Among the invited are fashion industry insiders, celebrities, and socialites. Runway shows are not ticketed events and are simply not accessible to the general public. I would be attending thanks to my childhood friend, Sonya.

Sonya and I had met in the fifth grade when she was "the new girl" in school. It was difficult for Sonya to fit in since most of the students already had established friendships with each other. I was her first real friend. Sonya was from Morocco. Since I loved *The Arabian Nights* and was very curious about Morocco and its culture, we had a natural bond. Sonya spoke several different languages including French, Italian, and Spanish, so she always seemed quite worldly to me.

Not surprisingly, Sonya ended up becoming a globe-trotting fashion photographer. Whenever she flew into New York, we would meet to catch up. The annual Spring/Summer Fashion Week in New York had become like our own personal ritual. I felt very fortunate to have a personal "in" to Fashion Week shows and events. As much as I enjoyed the shows, I was especially looking forward to seeing Sonya.

At previous shows, we had seen it all—models teetering down the runway in mile-high heels, nearly tripping off the catwalk, and breasts exposed due to wardrobe malfunctions. The first time you see it, it's a bit shocking, but the models always somehow managed to maintain their composure as they deftly pulled the offending item of clothing back into place and continued walking nonchalantly down a runway—all the while, their faces remaining devoid of emotional expression. But Fashion Week never gets old. How could one ever get tired of all the glamour, energy, excitement, pulsating music, beautiful models, and clothes?

On the first day of Fashion Week, my phone rang at 8:00 in the morning. Who would call at such an hour? I thought it certainly couldn't be Sonya. She would not call at this early hour, unless there was some major emergency. I looked at my phone and didn't recognize the number so I let it go to voicemail. As I headed over to a 10:00 fashion show that morning, I received a text message.

> 8:47 A.M. "Hi pretty lady. I just left you a message. I'm looking forward to seeing you on the side of the runway."

Then, I realized that the text message was from Gustav. He was probably the one who had left me a voicemail earlier. I had bumped into him at a Fashion Week party the night before. We had actually first met more than a year ago at a fashion-networking event. I remember noticing that he definitely had a unique personal sense of style. I never really knew the extent of his business or what real connections he had in the fashion industry. What he had told me seemed rather vague. We had met for drinks once but then he let it slip that he was married, so I decided not to encourage him.

Last night he told me that he was now divorced. I had conversed with him and decided to test the waters to find out if he was as connected as he had said he was. So, I asked him: "Are you going to the Marc Jacobs show tomorrow? I hear it is one of the hardest shows to get into. I'd love to go but I don't know of anyone able to get me in."

"Oh, you've never been to one of Marc's shows? You must go. I'll definitely be there," Gustav said.

"Well, do you think you can pull some strings and get me in to see the show?"

"No problem, I'll just bring you in with me," Gustav said confidently.

I now listened to the voicemail Gustav had left:

> "I'm here for the first show at 9:00 A.M. Haven't seen you around. Are you here yet? Call me. Let's figure out our game plan for the day."

As I listened to the message, I thought, did he actually think that I was going to spend the entire day with him attending fashion shows? That was a bit presumptuous on his part. Besides, I already had my own plans for the day. I had only talked to him about possibly going to the Marc Jacobs show together.

As I rushed into the 10:00 show, I felt my phone vibrate. It was another text message from Gustav:

10:02 A.M. Are you here yet? When will you be here? Can't wait to see you! Let me know when you're here.

When I arrived at the Carolina Herrera show, it was about to start so I quickly took a seat in the audience. I knew that Sonya would be squeezed into the press section preparing to shoot the show. We would find each other after the show. When the show ended, I went to find Sonya in the press section. When Sonya saw me, she squealed and we embraced like long-lost sisters.

"It's so great to see you!" I told her.

"It's always a good time when we get together," Sonya said.

"It really never gets old being here. It's always exciting!" I remarked.

It was 11:00 A.M. and my phone started vibrating again as we walked out of the show.

Gustav was calling again. This time I picked up. "Hi, sexy lady. I was thinking about you last night. Are you here yet? When am I going to get to see you?" he asked.

I was a bit taken aback by his overfamiliarity. "Well, actually I'm with one of my girlfriends now. We are planning to spend the day going to shows together."

"But when am I going to see you? Come and meet me for lunch."

"I can't exactly do that. I'm with my friend, Sonya, right now," I said feeling pressured.

"We're still on for Marc Jacobs—right? Let's meet right before the Marc Jacobs show at 3:00 P.M. I'll take care of everything," Gustav said with a hint of urgency in his voice.

"Yes, that sounds great," I said.

Gustav continued babbling about some of the shows he'd already seen that morning. Finally, when he ran out of air and had to take a breath, I quickly seized the opportunity to let him know that I would see him later at the Marc Jacobs show and ended the conversation.

I looked over at Sonya who was dressed in black from head to toe—her standard photographer's uniform. Her long, shiny, ebony hair, one of her best assets, was pulled back into a ponytail; she wore no makeup and had on wire-framed glasses. Dressed all in black like this, she looked like a ninja, I thought.

I had seen Sonya use some Jedi mind tricks to get past Fashion Week security and into some of the most exclusive runway shows. Even though Sonya had a press pass, the list keepers at the most exclusive shows would sometimes stop her and look her up and down deciding whether to let her in, but Sonya always got in. It made you wonder, just what were the criteria that got you in or "on the list?" There didn't always seem to be any rhyme or reason to it. But then I realized that it was one of two things, if they liked your overall look or if you simply exuded enough confidence so that they believed you had a legitimate reason to be there, then you'd be in.

"Who was that? Sounds like you couldn't get off of the phone quick enough," Sonya remarked. She had always been very perceptive.

"Oh, it was just some guy that I ran into yesterday. I had asked him if he could get me into the Marc Jacobs show today... he's been calling me nonstop since eight this morning! He's called me twice and sent me two text messages already!"

At 12:07 P.M., Gustav called again. I had kept my ringer off since I was running in and out of runway shows and now Sonya and I were going to go have lunch together.

At 1:15 P.M., while I was in another show with Sonya, Gustav left me yet another message.

At 2:36 P.M., he called just as Sonya and I had gotten out of another show. Glancing at my phone, I saw that I had a few missed calls from the now-familiar number. Gustav was calling me practically every hour. What was this guy expecting from me? I wondered as I reluctantly listened to my messages:

12:07 P.M. "Hi sugar, it's Gustav. Hope you're having a great day! I can't wait to see you later at the Armory. See you there at 3:00 P.M."

1:15 P.M. "Can't stop thinking about you. You are such an intelligent, classy lady. I will see you later at the Marc Jacobs show. Can't wait to see you!"

2:36 P.M. "I'm on my way to the Marc Jacobs show now. You should do your best to get here early. I'll be looking for you at the door."

Sonya raised her eyebrows as she looked over at me as I was listening to my messages. She saw that I was really starting to feel uneasy.

"This guy is calling me practically every hour now! I'm not so sure that I want to go to the Marc Jacobs show with him—even if he can get me in. I feel like I'm being stalked. Who knows what he really wants," I complained.

"Never mind him. Let's try to see if we can get into the Marc Jacobs show with my press credentials," Sonya said trying to reassure me.

We hailed a cab to go downtown. On the way there, my phone rang a few more times. Gustav was the last person I wanted to speak to.

When we finally arrived, we soon realized that we were too late. We had expected to see a long line of people waiting outside to get in, but only a small crowd of people was milling around. They were the people who had gotten shut out of the show. The show had already started.

I looked at my phone. Five missed calls. Two voice messages. Reluctantly, I dialed into my voicemail and listened.

2:45 P.M. "I'm almost there. Meet me there and we'll go in together."

2:51 P.M. "I'm about to go in, where are you? Are you on the way?" Gustav sounded a bit frantic above the voices in the crowd.

I decided to ignore his calls and just leave it at that. He'd get the message and I could just fade away, just as had happened a year ago.

That night he called and left another voicemail. I deleted it without listening to it.

The next day he sent me a series of text messages:

Tara, what happened to you yesterday? I will give you $100 if you would just write me back one word, just one word, that is all I want.

Hey Tara, I will give you $200 if you just text me one word, come on baby, just one word!

Baby! I will give you $300!

Honey, I will give $400 for just one word back from you. Please don't ignore me!

Tara, I will go up $500! That's a lot of money, don't you think?! Just one word from you baby! Just one response!

Okay, you're breaking my wallet! $600! Please respond! Just one word. You can do it! I know you can do it!

This is ridiculous! Okay, I will go up to $700! I know you are seeing these texts. Just send me one little word. That's all I need to know that it isn't over between the two of us!

Oh my God! Okay, $800! You happy? You're twisting my arm now! Just one word baby! I know you can do it!

Okay $900! You have to respond to me! Can't you see how crazy I am about you?!

Damn it to hell! $1,000! $1,000 of my hard-earned dollars! All for just one word from you! Baby! Honey! Sweetie! I need you! Don't let it end like this!

Those were the texts. I didn't respond and I was thinking about blocking his text messages, but didn't know how. Then, he wrote this email:

From: Gustav
To: Tara Reynolds
Subject: Hello?

====================

Tara, you have meant so much to me that words can't express it. My heart is broken and it has been stomped on over and over again by you ignoring me. I don't deserve to be treated like this. You are not acting like an adult. All I wanted was one word from you that it wasn't over. But no, that is too much to hope for from you. I am totally disappointed that you will never talk to me again. That thought is so depressing it just fills me with despair. It makes me not want to face the day knowing that you won't be a part of it. I know that you would never want to intentionally hurt me, but I can't see this as anything other than me getting hurt. Please, please, don't ignore me! I need to know that it isn't over between us. But no matter what you do, I wish you a happy life. I love you!

-Gustav

Somehow this guy had fallen desperately in love with me. I have had some guys fall for me right away, but this was ridiculous. He was in love with me? He didn't want it to be over? I didn't even know that there was something to get over. I didn't know what he would do next. So, I decided to lie. There was no way telling him the truth would work.

A few weeks after Fashion Week, Sonya and I met to catch up over a cup of coffee. This time Sonya was wearing a pastel-pink sweater, and smoky eye shadow that accentuated her dark brown eyes. Her long mane of ebony black hair, which I've admired since we first met, always looked naturally wavy and voluminous.

"So, whatever happened to your 'Fashion Week stalker'?" asked Sonya.

"Oh, you have no idea. He sent me texts constantly for a few days afterwards. It was nuts! Take a look at this," I said handing my phone over to Sonya.

"He seems like a compulsive texter," Sonya said as she strolled through Gustav's text messages and laughed.

"Then, he sent me an email saying that he was in love with me, begging that it not be over between us. So, I called him and told him that I didn't know how to respond to all his messages and email because I had a serious boyfriend now. He responded angrily and said that I should have told him that earlier. Then, I figured out how to block his number."

"I guess sometimes you have to lie to protect yourself, especially if you're dealing with a potential fatal attraction. Unfortunately, I think if you date long enough in this city, most women probably have some sort of a stalker story," Sonya said sympathetically.

Next!

(LUANA)

In my job as a senior financial analyst, I have gone through several assistants. I need people who know what they are doing. I am busy. Super busy. I really don't have the time to teach someone on the job. Right now, I have a great man as my assistant. He is married with kids and definitely not my type, which is perfect for an assistant. I don't believe in office romances. Office romances could be the equivalent of career suicide, so I try to keep business and pleasure separate.

At the Asia Society monthly Friday mixer, I met a man from New Zealand, Addison Robinson. He looked like he could be on the cover of *GQ* magazine, not just because of his looks, but also because of the way he was dressed. However, he seemed painfully shy. I found out that he was an urologist, which I assumed meant that he'd know exactly what to do with his dick. He was a classical music buff and said that he had an extensive classical music collection. So, I played along and asked if he would show me his collection, thinking that maybe the doctor really wanted to examine me.

He took me to his townhouse on the Upper East Side. As we stepped inside, I saw soaring ceilings, expensive artwork on the walls, and a spiral staircase. A huge chandelier hung in the foyer. Addison proceeded to give me a tour of all three floors, complete with five bedrooms and four and a half bathrooms. He even had an impeccably, professionally landscaped garden.

As I admired his home, I said, "I can't imagine that your urology practice is paying for all of this."

"Well, I do have some family money," Addison replied.

"Just some? It looks like you robbed Fort Knox! Does this work on all the ladies?" I teased.

"Actually, I don't bring that many women here," he said blushing.

"So, why don't you show me your music collection?" I asked.

I discovered that he really did have a huge collection of classical music. I asked him if he could play Ravel's "Bolero" and once he put on the CD, I suggested that we dance. Once he had his arms around me, I started kissing him gently, but he really didn't know how to kiss me back. He started doing peculiar pecking motions like he was a mama bird feeding its young.

I simply couldn't believe he could be worse in bed than his kissing, so I led him to his bedroom. As soon as we both got naked, I discovered he was hard. When it came to putting on the condom, he needed some help. I hope he doesn't do surgery because the man is all thumbs.

After some more fumbling around, he finally figured out how to get inside me and started doing some jerky movements like he was having a seizure. He came after just one minute and looked at me like I should be satisfied also. He gave me a few more bird pecks before getting up to go to the bathroom to throw away the condom. Then, he immediately turned on the shower. After ten minutes of showering, he exited the bathroom and found me already dressed. He gave me another bird peck, and then followed me as I got up to walk to his front door. I really saw no point in spending the night after the performance he just gave.

Once I got out the door, I couldn't stop thinking about how bad a kisser and lover this guy was. Even with all that money, I'm not sure how many women would come back for more. His lack of experience and horrific technique were proof that he really doesn't bring home that many women. I wouldn't be surprised if I was not the only woman to walk out of his house so soon after a screw with him.

How did I end up wasting time on such an amateur? My policy from now on is going to be that those lacking experience need not apply—just like the pathetic assistants at work that human resources have assigned to me in the past. Sorry to say that, but as a busy New Yorker, I don't have time to teach someone what to do at the office or in bed. All I have to say to that is, "Next!"

A man of Addison's age should've learned by now that a one-minute screw doesn't go over too well. It was so disappointing that I didn't even want to bother having another go at it. But let's get real! It's not that I necessarily want a Don Juan either. Well, maybe just for one night. What I want is someone who is somewhere in between my old boyfriend Gianni and the one-minute screw. Is that too much to ask?

Kiss First, Ask Questions Later

(FRANK)

The club in the Meatpacking District that I was at was packed, and I was in a make-out session with an attractive Latina who I had just met. I had approached her with a slight smile and she had smiled back at me. She was wearing a sleek dress with high slits that ran up along both sides of her hips, so that anyone could tell that she wasn't wearing any panties underneath. I was as attracted to her sense of style as I was to her curvy figure. With the briefest of introductions in the loud and dark club, I got a table and ordered a bottle of expensive champagne for both of us.

I discovered that her name was Olivia. As she was talking, with the music of the club blaring, I watched her sensuous lips without being able to hear what she was saying. Finally, I put my hand on the small of her back and then leaned in to kiss her for the first time. She was somewhat taken by surprise as she was in mid-sentence but immediately started kissing me back. After a half hour of making out, I asked her to come home with me, but she said that she was too tired and was staying over for the night at a friend's place on the Upper West Side. We made arrangements to meet up for dinner later that weekend. She was visiting from Vegas, so I suggested that we meet at Tavern on the Green, a quintessential New York institution known for its charming chandeliers and views of Central Park.

When Sunday arrived, Olivia showed up in a short emerald green dress that hugged her hips and showed off her legs. We kissed on the lips like old familiar lovers when we saw each other, but I realized that I really knew very little about her.

"We really didn't get a chance to talk at the club the other night. Loud clubs are good for making out and that's about it. So, I'm glad that you agreed to dinner," I said after we sat down at our table.

"That's true, but I discovered that you are a good kisser. I'm glad we met. This is a great choice. I have never been here before," said Olivia.

"This is one of my favorite spots in the city," I replied.

"Do you take a lot of women here?"

"Not a lot, but some."

The waiter came and we quickly looked at the menu.

"I'll have the Caesar salad and a chardonnay," Olivia told the waiter.

"I'll have the salmon and a chardonnay as well. I want the salmon medium. Thanks," I said giving the menus back to the waiter.

Turning the conversation back to her I asked, "So, Vegas? How long have you been living there?"

"I've been there most of my life. Practically lived in casinos growing up."

"Really, you must have some stories to tell about how you found your way around the gambling age limit," I joked.

"No, it's not like that. I wasn't a delinquent or anything. My dad was a pit boss at one of the casinos on the strip. But enough about me, why aren't you already married? Or have you been married before?" Olivia asked abruptly.

"I guess I haven't found the right person yet," I responded.

"But you are in your early forties. That's not really an answer," Olivia continued to probe.

"Yes, it is an answer if it is the truth."

"No, it isn't. There has to be a reason why you never got married. Every guy I've dated who is your age and not married has a secret reason why he isn't married. Some are afraid of commitment, those are the good ones, but at least that's a good reason for not getting married. The bad ones are those who are still attached to their mommy, can't get it up anymore, have a small dick, have no money, are in denial about being gay, or even weirder stuff than that."

"Man, you are cynical. Well, why aren't you married yet? You are not exactly in your twenties," I responded somewhat annoyed.

"Don't get defensive. I just really want to know the truth. Not some bullshit answer as to why you never got married," Olivia demanded.

"Once again, why haven't YOU ever gotten married?" I repeated.

"I guess I haven't found the right person yet."

"Man, is that a crock of bull. When I say the same thing, I am hiding some weird reason. You say it and you are the beacon of truth."

"I can't help it. With women it IS the truth. With men it is bullshit to say they haven't found the right person yet," Olivia said with an air of authority.

"I have to say that your view sounds very sexist," I said.

"Women can't be sexist. Only men can be sexist."

"Are you kidding me? That is such bullshit!"

"Don't be angry because I am saying the truth."

"Your truth... not THE truth," I responded in a harsh tone. "Do you get many second dates?"

"You have to be worthy to get a second date with me. I have some rules. I could go Dutch on the first date, but no kiss goodnight, only a handshake. Well, what happened with you the other night doesn't count. I was drunk. But on the second date, the man has to pay and I will kiss him on the cheek. On the third date, I will kiss him on the lips but no making out. I need the man to say he loves me before I will let him touch me anywhere. For sex, he needs to have met my parents and two sisters," Olivia said with conviction.

"Well, my question, 'Do you get many second dates?' was both rhetorical and sarcastic. What's with all these rules? Do you even care at all about what the man wants?"

"Of course I care. If I am home with my boyfriend, I let him have whatever he wants from my fridge."

"Wow! Do you even have food in your fridge?" I asked.

"No, I don't. I don't cook. Why should I have to cook? I never had to cook, we always got our food comped. But what does that have to do with anything?"

"So, what do you do when men don't want to abide by your rules?"

"I move on," Olivia shot back.

"If you want somebody to boss around, that's not me. I am not a doormat," I said in a matter-of-fact tone.

"I never said I wanted a doormat. I just want someone who follows my rules."

"I think you just gave the definition of what a doormat is," I responded.

"Well, I guess it is time for me to move on then," Olivia said in an annoyed tone.

Olivia called the waiter over and told him not to bother bringing her food, but to wrap it up so that she could take it to go.

As she got up to leave, I couldn't help myself and felt compelled to say one last thing. "Thanks for saving me the trouble because I need more than just having imaginary food from your refrigerator."

Olivia gave me a dirty look and left the restaurant. The waiter came over to hand me the bill and with a wry smile on my face, I told the waiter, "Next time I'll make sure that I really talk to the woman before I kiss her."

Sexy for a Day

(MONTOYA, Nine, Luana)

Esme was only going to stay with me for the weekend. She was the girlfriend of my cousin, Carlos, who lived in Ibiza, which some would claim is the "partying capital" of Spain. Carlos and Esme were both really into the Ibiza club scene. In fact, that's how they had met. Carlos was the son of my father's brother. While I grew up in London with a Spanish father and a British mother, Carlos had grown up in Madrid and both of his parents were Spanish.

When I went to JFK airport to pick Esme up, I spotted her immediately even though I had not met her before. Carlos had told me to look for the sexiest woman in the airport, and he definitely wasn't exaggerating. She was sex on a stick, with lovely long legs and two perky melon-sized... uh you get the picture.

Carlos himself was a good-looking guy at twenty-five years old, but having Esme as a girlfriend was hitting the jackpot. I'd say she was about a natural C cup with long wavy black hair, brown eyes, and curves in all the right places. But the kicker was her flawless face. Dressed casually in a T-shirt and jeans, wearing no makeup, she looked like a teenager, though she was twenty-one.

Esme was to stay in my spare bedroom. Most of the weekend she wanted to visit museums, since she was into art. So, she went to the Met, the MoMA, and the Frick. But on Saturday night, I had invited her to go with me to Nine's annual Halloween party. She had been throwing the party in her flat for years. I have always loved Halloween in New York City. It was the one day of the year that women who were normally conservatively dressed, all prim and proper, would be scantily clad in some Halloween outfit. They would be sexy for a day. And there were always some women who pushed the envelope wearing outfits that showed off some of their naughty bits.

Esme had said she would meet me directly at Nine's flat. Approximately forty people were in Nine's Union Square apartment dressed in various Halloween costumes. Frank was dressed as Count Dracula, Tara was showing a lot of leg as the Egyptian Queen Nefertiti, and Nine was dressed in a short little angel costume complete with wings. Roxanne was dressed as Little Bo Peep, which seemed apt because her dress was so short and low cut that every time she bent over; it was as if she was giving all the men a free peep show.

Luana was wearing a blonde wig and dressed as Eve (as in Adam and Eve). She had a very realistic looking serpent wrapped around her bare shoulders with leaves strategically placed to cover her private parts. Katia came dressed in a flight attendant's uniform that had a plunging neckline revealing her ample cleavage and the words "Fly Me" embroidered on one of the breast pockets. I was dressed as a New York City cop in a full navy blue uniform, complete with a fake badge and police baton.

When Esme came into the apartment, she was wearing a long coat so I didn't initially see her Halloween costume. But when she took off her coat, I was shocked to see her wearing a micro-thong bikini and not much else. The thong was literally one blue string in the front that didn't cover up her vadge and rode up her bum in the back. On top she had two gold badges strategically placed to cover her nips. Her torso and vadge were covered in glittery navy blue body paint and she wore a matching cap and a pair of handcuffs on her left wrist.

"What in heaven's name are you supposed to be?" I blurted out when I saw her.

"I am a New York City cop like you, partner. Can't you tell from the handcuffs, my badges, and the blue cap?" she asked innocently.

"This is America, not Ibiza," I responded.

She was essentially nude and was the center of attention the entire night. Several women rolled their eyes at me as they walked past us. Frank patted me on the back as he gave me a wink and a sly smile. Tara was busy talking with some guy dressed as a samurai. But Nine looked absolutely furious. Luana was the only woman who was friendly to Esme and talked to her most of the night comparing exercise regimens. I felt as though I had to keep an eye on Esme that night so I spent most of the night talking to both Luana and Esme. When Esme excused herself to go to the restroom, it gave me a chance to talk one-on-one with Luana.

"I know that tonight most people's eyes are on Esme and her scandalous costume. But your costume doesn't leave much to the imagination either," I said admiring her strategically placed leaves, marveling at how they had managed to stay in place all night.

"And I like a man in uniform," Luana said suggestively. "There is something so authoritative about a man in uniform."

"Interesting that you say that because I feel like I am Esme's bodyguard, keeping the men here from messing with her. I promised my cousin, Carlos, that I'd look after her."

Esme came back to join our conversation. As she turned around, both of us saw an obvious hand print on her bum where blue glittery body paint had been rubbed off. Luana and I exchanged looks at the sight. Luana laughed, and I almost laughed, but it didn't seem right to do so.

"I think you should dust her butt for fingerprints to find out who's responsible for that," Luana said to me still laughing.

Hearing Luana laughing, Esme turned around and said, "What's so funny?" She was completely oblivious.

"My dear, you have a handprint on your arse. It looks like some of your body paint there has been rubbed off. I don't know who the offending party is, and I don't want to get into it, so I think it's time to go home," I said firmly to Esme.

I went to get her coat and put it over her shoulders to cover up the offending evidence. Then, I said my goodbyes to Luana, Frank, Tara, Katia, Roxanne, and Nine. Esme and I went straight back to my place since she had a flight the next day. The following afternoon, I took her to JFK, to see her off and on her way back to my lucky cousin Carlos.

Later that same day, Nine texted me saying that she wanted to meet me for a drink. We agreed to meet at Terra Blues in the Village. I told her to meet me at 9:30 that evening, which would give us a chance to talk in-between the blues sets at the club. When I saw Nine, I could tell that she seemed to be upset with me because she only gave me a hug, but no kiss on the check as she usually did. As soon as we sat down, she blurted out: "Why did you bring a nude underage woman to my party?! You're lucky you weren't arrested!"

"Wait a minute! She wasn't underage. Do you think I'm mad as a hatter? She's twenty-one."

"But she was nude! Nude! In my apartment!"

Nine surprised me with her strong reaction. "I saw other women rolling their eyes at me probably thinking who was this woman that I'd brought to your party? But they weren't furious like you. Why are you so upset?"

"Why?"

"Yes, why?"

"Why?" she repeated.

"Is there an echo in this bar? Nine, yes, why?"

"Well, first of all, no one would have said anything to you about it because that would have just caused a scene. Besides, you shouldn't be with anyone that young."

"I wasn't. I told you at the party when I introduced her to you that she is my cousin's girlfriend," I insisted.

"I know," she seemed to be at a loss for words for a moment. Then, she added. "But other people at the party didn't know. You have no business being with anyone that young, you're thirty-six years old! Why are you with all these young chicks? At least, be with someone near my age."

"Seriously, my dear, what is the difference between someone who's twenty-six like you and a twenty-one year old?"

Again, she was furious, "There is a world of difference between a twenty-six year old and a twenty-one year old. That's five years of maturity."

"Nine, I don't see the issue at all unless you're telling me that you don't want me to date anyone younger than you. Is that it?"

"Well, yes. Yes. Don't date anyone younger than me. It isn't right! They're jailbait. You could wind up in jail!"

"Nine, my dear, I have never been with anyone underage. Are you jealous? Nine, I thought we always had a sibling-type relationship?"

"We do! We do. It isn't jealousy."

"I can see why any woman would be jealous of Esme," I said trying to diffuse the tension between us. "But seriously, I think that your name is fitting because I don't believe that any woman is a perfect ten, and the closest any woman can come to perfection is a nine," I said finally feeling like I was no longer under attack by Nine. "And love, you are definitely a nine."

"Maybe it is similar to a divorced dad who is now dating someone as young as his daughter. It isn't jealousy. It just makes me feel uncomfortable."

"Hey, I'm only ten years older than you. I'm hardly old enough to be your dad," I kidded.

"Okay, you're more like an older brother to me."

"I get it now, love, don't get your knickers in a twist. I won't date anyone under twenty-six years old from this day forward. You mean the world to me."

Nine gave me a big hug as she said, "Thanks Montoya. I love you."

"Love you too," I said hugging her back and giving her a kiss on the cheek.

The Keeper

(TARA and Luana)

One relationship in my life was sacred. When I found it, I knew that this was the one, a real keeper. I needed someone who I could count on and trust. The longest relationship had lasted nearly four years, but when he had moved out of the state, I didn't know where to turn.

He had been recommended by a friend who had since also moved to another state. He was a middle-aged Japanese man, who didn't speak English very well. The first time I went to him, I painstakingly explained to him how I wanted my hair cut, and I watched his every snip like a hawk. He had patiently cut my hair periodically pausing to ask, "This okay?" And I felt assured. That was the extent of our conversations.

I did not want just anyone messing with my hair. Asian hair is notoriously hard to cut and finding the right hairdresser is not an easy feat. For me, bad haircuts are traumatizing—and they would take at least a month to grow out. I had tried a few expensive salons, but I was still not satisfied with the results. It was agonizing for me to have to start over again. Each time, I'd have to carefully communicate my expectations and then hope not to be disappointed with the results.

Finally, out of frustration one day, I just walked into a mid-priced hair salon chain and asked for a hairdresser who was good with Asian hair. That is how I had met Lenora "Sassy" Ramirez last month.

Sassy was a voluptuous Latina babe who spoke with a New York accent to match her straight-talking style. I immediately noticed that she had a tattoo of the Chinese character "love" on her inner wrist. It was one of the few Chinese characters that I knew. During our initial consultation, Sassy asked me what I wanted her to do with my hair. Did I know exactly how I wanted her to cut my hair or was I ready to try something different? I went through the standard description: long bangs, long layers throughout to give my hair a nice shape and volume, but not too short, long enough so that my hair could still be pulled back into a ponytail or styled into an updo.

Sassy immediately launched into a conversation as she combed through my hair. "So, how has your week been? Anything fun planned for the weekend?" Sassy asked as I noticed that her long, hot pink, rhinestone-tipped nails, matched her skintight fuchsia and black leopard print dress.

"Oh, nothing out of the ordinary. I don't always have plans for the weekend," I replied. I was usually reserved when talking about my personal life, especially to strangers. In fact, there were some things that I just didn't discuss, even with my close friends.

"I have a gig on Saturday. Did I tell you that I'm also a singer?" Sassy said cheerily as she pinned up a section of my hair and started cutting.

That explained a few things, I thought. Sassy kind of sounded like a stage name, which matched her fun, girlie style. Dressed up in hot pink, from head to toe, she looked like a real life Barbie doll. Sassy stopped cutting and unpinned the top layer of my hair as she said, "And hopefully, I'm going to see my man this weekend, too. But who knows? I sent him a text message the other day and he said 'maybe,' but I haven't been able to reach him by phone lately. I'm not sure what's up with that!"

What Sassy said struck a chord in me and I responded, "Oh, I can relate to that. Actually, with this guy I'm seeing right now, it's sometimes hard for me to get in contact with him. He doesn't always respond to my text messages right away. But when I see him, it's all good. He always says what a great time he has with me and asks when he can see me again. But then, he doesn't always follow up. Come to think of it, we haven't made any plans to meet up yet this weekend."

"Men! Maybe we are just making it too easy for them and they get lazy and comfortable. Why do any work when the woman has everything all planned out?" Sassy remarked.

The question hung in the air as Sassy continued cutting and soon she was blow drying my hair.

The guy I had been seeing lately was Willem, and our connection was electric. Willem was dreamy. He was one of the most cultured, artistic men I'd ever dated. He was a sculptor and a professional massage therapist. The first time we kissed, I could tell that he knew what he was doing. He was such a good kisser that kissing him was almost like foreplay. Kissing him always put me in the mood. It would make me forget everything—even if he hadn't returned my calls or if I hadn't seen him in a few days.

When we kissed, I felt as though my lips melted into his. And the way he touched me made me feel so relaxed and excited at the same time. It was a bit like the tension and pleasure that one feels as if she is being tickled or anticipates being tickled. If you're ticklish, you'll know exactly what that means. Just the mere suggestion or "threat" of being tickled creates a giddy sensation and makes you squirm.

In the beginning, our dates usually consisted of going to plays, classical music concerts, and late night dinners. It was all terribly romantic. He would bring me flowers for no reason at all. Once, as we were walking back to his place at the end of a date, he stopped at a flower stand and said, "Pick something out. I want to buy you some flowers. You look so gorgeous tonight." As he said this, he hugged me, lifting me up in the air off my feet. And the sex was amazing. Maybe it was because the foreplay had started long before we even made it to the bedroom, with music concerts, the flowers, and romantic dinners.

Sassy was now dry cutting my hair and when it was all done, it looked amazing. I was impressed, "It looks great!" I told her.

On the way home from the salon, Sassy's remarks about men being lazy and getting comfortable gave me pause. Lately, I had started wondering. Though Willem and I have had these amazing dates, he would sometimes disappear for a day or two afterward. And he didn't always pick up my phone calls.

His business card only had an email address, his website, and a phone number. He didn't have an office because he said that he made house calls. It was easier that way and his clients seemed to like the convenience. Having treatments at home offered the added bonus of prolonging the relaxation effect. Afterwards, his clients didn't have to get all dressed again and go home, he explained. I had seen his foldable massage table and the way he'd explained it seemed to make sense. I'd once had an acupuncturist who made house calls so it didn't seem strange at all.

As I thought about it, I realized that he hadn't initiated any dates in a while. I had planned our last few dates. We'd gone to see a live band, and on another night we went out dancing. Every time we saw each other, he'd say how much he was looking forward to seeing me again and that we should get together soon. But then, he didn't follow up. Sometimes he'd call or text me at odd hours, to see if I was home. If I was, he'd stop by and spend the night.

I was tired of being the one to do all the work, of constantly waiting for Willem to respond to my messages, and his unpredictable late night messages and visits. So, I decided to just wait and see what would happen if I didn't make any plans or initiate something. I had told him that I was planning to go to a friend's birthday party on Saturday, but Willem hadn't said anything about accompanying me to it all week and the weekend was fast approaching.

That Friday I decided to just stay in. Around 1 A.M. in the morning, Willem texted me asking what I was up to. After a few suggestive messages flew back and forth, as was the customary late night dance of text messages, I was expecting him to say he'd stop by. But Willem wrote that he wasn't going to stop by but that he'd see me tomorrow night at the birthday party. What a huge tease he'd been! I was kind of annoyed. I had mentioned the party to him a week ago but had already planned to go by myself since I hadn't heard back from him.

The following night I only knew that Willem would eventually turn up at the party, which was at some trendy little spot on the Lower East Side. He had not said what time he'd be there and we had not even made plans to meet up beforehand. About an hour after I had arrived, I realized that Willem still hadn't arrived. Soon, I lost track of the time as I started to enjoy the scene without him.

When Willem walked in, I was chatting with Luana. Seeing him walk over to me, Luana excused herself by saying that she needed to talk to someone she hadn't seen in a while. Later on in the evening, when Willem was not by my side, Luana reappeared, "So where's your man?"

"Getting a drink and talking to the boys over there with Frank and Montoya," I said.

"I think I should tell you that I've met Willem before. He's a personal masseur—right?"

"Yes. How did you meet? Don't tell me that you and he…" I paused, bracing myself for the answer.

"Well no, not exactly. Ummm, let's just say that he offers a few very special services that are not officially advertised on his website. I used to call him 'Mr. Happy Ending'… if you get my drift. Just ask him. It's the thing that he's in the most demand for and what he gets paid the most for."

I didn't know what to think or how I was going to broach the topic with Willem because I knew that he and I would probably leave together and end up at my place. Sure enough, at the end of the night, we hailed a cab back to my place.

"Baby, you looked so gorgeous tonight, I just wanted to do this all night," Willem said as he leaned in to kiss me. I gave in and kissed him back, feeling the speed of the cab pickup. I loved kissing Willem, but in the back of my mind I thought of what Luana had said to me about him. So, by the time the cab had arrived at my place, I had figured out what to say to him.

Once we were in my apartment, Willem started undressing me. Soon we were on the bed and he was running his hands up and down my body "Mmm, you are so good at that, you really know how to touch me," I told him. I knew what was coming next as Willem's hand slid down my hips to my thighs. Before I let him go any further I said, "I know what you are going to do next and you are very good at that. It is quite a skill and I'll bet that there are women who would pay top dollar for your magic fingers to give them moments of ecstasy. Is that a service that you've ever offered to your female clients?"

"No," Willem said as his fingers started reaching between my legs.

I knew that I had to stop him before things went too far, so I put my hand on his stopping him as I asked, "Well, have you ever been asked by a client to do this?"

"Well, if you put it that way. Yes," Willem answered.

"Really?! You've done that?" I looked at him feeling stunned.

"But that was only for very special clients, and I don't do that anymore," Willem said trying to reassure me. "That's in the past. I'm not going to do anything to mess up our relationship," he said as he started kissing me, taking my mind off of everything. I gave in. I had wanted him since the other night when he had sexted me at 1 A.M.

The next morning I woke up with Willem beside me. Our problems were certainly not in the bedroom. I just could not seem to resist him. While he was still sleeping, I wondered if I should keep him around or not, and how many other women he had pleasured for money.

A Miss and a Hit

(FRANK and MONTOYA)

Frank and Montoya were sitting at a bikini bar downtown watching a heavyweight boxing match on one of the many TV screens in the bar. Several women dressed in skimpy bikinis and high heels were serving the mostly male customers. Along the bar, men in suits sat relaxing and enjoying the match and the eye candy probably after having worked several long hours. A group of women in business attire were also there. One had to wonder if the women were there to be picked up or were also just relaxing after a hard day.

Montoya's Story:

As was our custom, Frank and I would grab a drink and share our dating adventures or in some cases, misadventures. I could tell that Frank had a story to tell because he wasn't paying as much attention as he usually did to the ladies behind the bar.

The bartender, Raven, who I knew by name, had long dark hair to match her name. She spoke with a Midwestern accent and was wearing a lime green bikini, which showed off her tanned skin, slender figure, and ample D-cup bosoms. Frank ordered some chicken fingers and was drinking a beer while I was having a gin tonic with two wedges of lime.

"You're never going to believe what happened on the date that I had last night!" Frank said.

"So, what happened? Did you shag her?" I asked.

Frank took a quick sip of his beer and said, "No, well, the date didn't exactly go as planned."

"Oh really?"

"No, but something even better happened," Frank said.

"Of course," I said with raised eyebrows anticipating the epic saga of Frank's date.

"The woman I had the date with—this woman Dara—boy was I wrong about her."

"How did the two of you meet?" I asked.

"I met her at my gym last week. You know I can't swim, but I was at the pool area having a Red Bull while checking out the talent. Then I saw her come out of the women's dressing room wearing this sexy red bikini and she dove right into the pool. What an unbelievable body! When she finished her swim and got out of the pool, I went over to her to make a quick introduction. I got her number and made plans to have dinner with her. But when she showed up for the date, her look kind of disgusted me."

"Come on mate. After seeing her in a bikini, how can you be surprised by how she looks?"

"She showed up dressed in an oversized T-shirt, jeans and gym shoes. And her hair looked kind of greasy. She kept scratching her head, and I swear that I saw a few big chunks of dandruff stuck in her hair," Frank responded.

"So, she was scratching like an ape or something? Maybe her shower was broken. You should have offered to take her somewhere to get a nice clean shower," I ribbed Frank.

"Yeah right. Like that's a good line to use on a first date. I'd like to see you work that into a conversation. Actually, I think that you are one of the few people who could manage to do that without seeming like a pervert."

"What can I say? I guess it's one of my talents," I said in acknowledgment.

"Man, I wanted to get out of there before the entree even arrived."

"Come on. How bad could it have been?"

Frank's Story:

So, I was on this date with this woman Dara. I knew the woman had a body to die for, though you wouldn't have been able to tell by looking at her then. I wondered why she had shown up dressed the way she was. I mean, she knew what kind of a place I had planned to take her to for dinner. It was not some diner.

I continued telling Montoya about my date with Dara, "There she was having a beer before dinner and she burped a few times. No, actually, she belched. It was so unladylike."

"Blame it on the beer," Montoya said chuckling.

"We were at an amazing steakhouse that I've been wanting to go to. It wasn't easy to get a reservation there and I wasn't about to pass up a great steak, so, I thought I'm here, I've ordered, I'll at least stick it out and try out the steak."

"I'm telling you, if you could've just gotten her out of those clothes and into a shower, then everything would've been alright," Montoya teased.

"Well, it gets better. Another couple was sitting near us. And when their check came, we could overhear the guy say to the girl, 'Mind if we go Dutch?' I thought maybe they were on their first date or something. Seeing this, Dara tapped me on the hand and said loudly so that everyone could hear, 'Can you believe this asshole? What kind of jerk expects the woman to pay for half the meal?'"

"Sounds like a sticky situation," Montoya said.

"The guy, who was middle-aged, turned to Dara and said, 'No offense lady, but what business is this of yours?' Dara responded angrily, 'Men should always pay for dinner! No exceptions!' Then, the woman who was with the man spoke up and said, 'Why don't you mind your own business? We aren't on a date. He and I are friends. Why don't you pay attention to your own business and while you're at it, maybe you should think about how you could show up dressed like that for a place like this? And another thing, you should really mind your table manners, belching the way you did.' "

"It sounds like it just went from bad to worse," Montoya said.

"Right. As the couple were getting up to leave, Dara looked at me and yelled, 'Aren't you going to speak up?! How can you let the both of them speak to me like that?' "

"Why is it that you always seem to end up with these demanding women?" Montoya observed.

"Yeah, well, I tried to get Dara to calm down and said, 'Dara, they are right. Why are you getting involved in their business?' She was furious and said, 'How dare you tell me they are right? A man should always pay for dinner!' So, I said to her, 'Did you hear at all what they said? They are friends, not on a date.' Then, she said, 'And can you believe they had the nerve to tell me how I should dress?' To that I said, 'Sorry, but I'd have to say that I agree with them about the way that you are dressed.' As soon as I said this, I knew the date would end very abruptly. But by that point, I didn't care anymore. Dara went ballistic, got up and stormed out of the restaurant leaving me there alone and with the bill, of course."

"Sorry to hear that, but when or how did things turn around?" Montoya asked. "I thought you said that something better happened."

I took a sip of my beer and continued, "After Dara left, I decided to stay to eat my steak in peace. The waitress came over and asked, 'Is there anything I can get for you, sir?' I said to her, 'How about a new date?' But I was just joking. She said, 'I just saw what happened and heard the entire thing. I thought you handled that very well. Your date was totally unreasonable and rude. Did you know she would show up dressed like that?' I told her, 'Believe it or not, I met my date at a pool so she was in a bikini when we met. I had never seen her fully dressed.' Then the waitress, whose name was Lissette said, 'If you'd like a new date, maybe I could help you with that order? Would you like to grab a drink with me after my shift is over? I'm getting off in an hour.' "

"Brilliant," Montoya said. "It's always amazing to me how you're able to get into these interesting situations."

"Lissette was a hottie and she had a really great smile. She was wearing a tight little black dress and had really nice legs. She was definitely in great shape and not afraid to show it. I was almost done with my meal so, I said, 'Sure, but what am I going to do for an hour?' She suggested that I have a drink while waiting for her in the employees' lounge. When she was finished with her shift, she came and sat with me in the employees' lounge and we talked for a while. She was fun, very flirtatious, and really sexy. Somehow, I got the impression that she knew what she was doing and that maybe she'd done this before."

"I think I can see where this is going," Montoya said as he reached to take a sip of his drink.

"Lissette said to me, 'Your date looked like a hot mess. I guess she must have looked really good in that bikini when you met.' "

"And then I said to Lissette, 'I bet you also would look good in a bikini.' That's when I leaned in and kissed her. I wanted to jump her right there. We were alone in the lounge and I was going for her bra when we heard people in the kitchen. It sounded like they were headed to the lounge. She was afraid of getting caught, so she stopped me and said, 'Let's go back to my place.' We got a cab over to her apartment. Thankfully, it was not too far away because I was ready to practically do her in the cab."

Montoya's Story:
"So, how was it?"

"She gave me head and then we had sex. It was a satisfying feel-good lay. It definitely more than made up for the debacle with Dara," Frank said as he picked up a chicken finger, which by this time was probably cold.

"And what happened with the belching bikini girl?" I asked.

Frank put his hand under his neck and did a slitting-throat motion, "That relationship was as dead as dead could be. I'd turned off my phone in case Dara tried to call and curse me out. After I got home, I blocked her number and deleted her email address."

I reached for my G and T and said, "When you go on these dates, you never know if it will be a hit or a miss. In this case you had a miss with Dara and a hit with Lissette. It amazes me how you are able to turn these situations around. Good job." I raised my G and T and Frank raised his glass of beer.

"I'll drink to that," Frank said as we clinked our glasses and downed our drinks.

Just then Raven came by and asked, "So, do you guys want another round?"

"Sure. Same drinks as before," I said. "Raven, this is my friend, Frank." Frank extended his hand and Raven shook it. "He was just telling me his sad tale of how his date walked out on him at a restaurant."

"That is terrible," Raven said looking at Frank. "You seem like a nice guy."

"He is. I absolutely vouch for his character. So, Raven, how about you and one of your friends joining us at this great hotel bar that is one block away when your shift ends?"

"Sounds good. I will ask around and see who is available," Raven said as she walked down to the other end of the bar. This time Frank noticed her and was checking out her body.

"So?" I said smiling. "Once again, like Dara, you've only seen Raven in her bikini."

"And you're suggesting going to a hotel bar? With rooms upstairs? You crazy Brit."

"You are not the only one who knows how to turn a situation around," I said grinning.

BOOK 1

WINTER

Keeping it Going

(TARA and Luana)

I went to get my monthly haircut with Sassy. As usual, Sassy immediately launched into conversation as she picked up her scissors. "I've been reading this book, called *Act Like A Lady, Think Like a Man* by Steve Harvey, which I'd highly recommend. It's about how women should have more self-respect and never settle for a man treating her any less than a lady. It's so important to set the tone from the beginning of the relationship and to stick to it so that the man knows that he can't get away with anything," Sassy said as she snipped away.

"You're going to have to write down the title of that book for me."

"Sure, maybe I can even lend you my copy. A few months ago, I finally gave this guy that I've been with for AGES the heave ho, and recently I met someone new, but I'm taking it slow. I told the new guy that I want to go slow, and you know what, it is driving him crazy. He's calling me all the time and asking to see me, but I am not giving in. So, what's new with you? Is that same guy you told me about still in the picture?" Sassy asked me.

I had tried to break up with Willem a few times because of his disappearing acts. He didn't always return my calls, or make plans to see me in advance. Then, there were his late night booty calls, which were kind of exciting in the beginning, but I had started to feel like he was not exactly available when I wanted him, and that maybe he was just getting a bit too comfortable in the relationship. I wished that he would put a bit more effort into the relationship.

But he would always come back around, and I would forget all of this when we were together.

"Well, I did try to break up with him but now... we are kind of trying to sort things out," I said.

"What does that mean?" Sassy asked with a hint of skepticism.

"We are kind of off and on again."

"I see, it's THAT good, is it?"

"Yeah, I saw him again recently and well one thing kind of led to another. I guess there's a part of me that just can't seem to resist him," I said feeling embarrassed for admitting my weakness for him. None of my friends really knew about this. In fact, they probably assumed it was over because they had heard me express my frustrations with Willem and they hadn't seen me with him in a while. So, it was like we were carrying on a secret little affair, which made it all the more exciting. "I couldn't help it. I just gave in and we both realized that we still have so many feelings for each other." It felt liberating to be able to tell Sassy.

"Listen, honey, even though there aren't any issues in the bedroom, I don't think you should be messing with an ex for too long. There's a reason why he's your ex," Sassy cautioned.

After I was done with my haircut, I met up with Luana for a late brunch at a little French café in the West Village. Once we placed our orders, Luana launched right into conversation.

"So, whatever happened to Willem? I haven't seen the two of you together recently. I'm sorry that I was the one who had to break the news to you about him. I hope that didn't weird you out too much, but I thought you should know."

"Yeah, well, I asked him about it and he told me that it was all in the past," I said. I knew that Luana would not judge me so I admitted the situation to her, "I have been seeing him off and on."

"Oh really? That doesn't sound like you are exactly sure about him." Luana paused. "Tara, I think you should know that what I told you about him, what he does, that's not in his past. I know quite a few of his past and present clients. Sorry to have to again be the messenger of bad news. I was going to make an appointment to see him, but I wanted to talk to you because I wasn't sure if things were over between the two of you," Luana informed me.

I knew that Luana wouldn't lie about something like this. "Well, then, that means that Willem basically lied to me. And now you are asking me if it's okay for you to see him because you'd like to have one of his 'happy ending' specials?" I responded.

"Oh no. No way, especially since I know that you and Willem are still an item. However, if I were to get a massage from him, it would've probably led to a 'happy ending.' But I can always find another masseur or a lover to satisfy my needs," Luana said confidently.

"Thanks for letting me know about all this. I think I need to figure out what to do about this," I said.

Later that evening, as I was alone in my apartment, I thought about whether I could deal with what Willem did for a living, and whether I could really trust him. I wondered about the special clients he was working overtime to service. Just how many women were his skillful hands pleasing? There was no point in confronting him about this because he had already lied to me. I decided that I'd have to take a break from him to get a clearer perspective on things.

More Than I Could Handle

(MONTOYA and Tara)

I have had many women with strong libidos, but none could compare to Gemma. She was young by my standards, at twenty-six years old. As I had promised Nine, I wouldn't date anyone younger than her, and Gemma was exactly Nine's age. Gemma was a brunette, originally from Los Angeles, with fair skin and several body piercings including one in each nipple. The best one for me was the one in her tongue, which enhanced her blow job skills.

Since she was living at her aunt's place on Staten Island, we often ended up back at my flat. So, I decided to just give her a set of keys. Gemma made herself at home by immediately cooking up a storm. I never cook so my kitchen never got as much action as it did as when Gemma was around. I didn't mind. She was an amazing cook. I have never seen my fridge so full of food and leftovers. It was as if she was preparing for the apocalypse.

She was quite the sex kitten or more like a sex tiger. She was always in the mood, so we often spent the whole weekend holed up in my flat, not that I'm complaining. I had a sneaking suspicion that she cooked so much so that we would never have to leave my flat. We'd have sex, refuel on her cooking, and go at it again. Sometimes as I slept, I felt Gemma giving me some sort of a blow job or hand job to the point of getting me hard; then, I would wake up to find her riding me in the woman-on-top position. I had to constantly remind her to put a condom on me.

Last week, I came home from work, took off my suit and went to my closet to hang it up when I realized that half of what had been in there was now gone. Then, I went to my dresser to get a T-shirt and discovered that half of the drawers had been cleaned out.

"Gemma, what did you do with half of my suits and my T-shirts?"

"I did a little spring cleaning; besides, it's time for a new wardrobe for you. I bought you some replacements."

I was not completely surprised that she had done this. She ran her own business as a personal organizer, and she viewed my flat as a work in progress. She did have quite a knack for organizing spaces. At her suggestion, I had rearranged some of the furniture in my apartment and it did feel much more spacious afterward.

Lately, she had been obsessively organizing everything. First, it was the food in the fridge. Each container of leftover food she'd prepared was carefully labeled to indicate its contents and the date. Then, it was my personal objects. She alphabetized all of my books by the author's last name, organized my wardrobe by color palette, and then organized every item in my kitchen.

"I appreciate what you are trying to do, but you can't just do this sort of thing without telling me, or more importantly asking me."

"It's okay. You can thank me later. It's all been taken care of. I donated everything to Goodwill this morning."

"Donated everything to Goodwill?!" I repeated her words back trying to take in what she just told me.

I thought about the first suit that my Mum had bought me when I graduated from uni. I'd worn it to my first job interview; it was also my first designer suit. My varsity T-shirts were also gone. Everything was gone. She had crossed the line. I had given her a set of keys for convenience sake and she had interpreted that as me giving her power of attorney over my flat. It felt like she was taking over my life.

So, I told her as gently and firmly as I could, that she had gone too far. I didn't know what she was going to do next. I couldn't trust her. I asked her to give me back her keys to my apartment. She did not take my suggestion well. She had tears in her eyes as I suggested that we take a break from each other for a while.

I had been so wrapped up with Gemma that I had missed out on several events and was late on returning emails and phone calls. People wondered where I had been. But I didn't want to say that I had entered a sex-crazed Bermuda Triangle of sorts where I was fed and shagged repeatedly. Not a bad way to go, but not something you want to publicize.

Once I got my keys back, I responded to a text from Tara who was wondering where I'd disappeared to. That made me realize that I'd really let things get out of hand. So, I got in touch with Tara and made plans to meet up with her a few days later.

Tara agreed to meet me uptown at a bar in my neighborhood and that's when I told her that Gemma and I had broken up. When Tara heard this, she asked, "What's the problem? She was super cute. The two of you seemed good together. She cooked for you all the time, reorganized your flat, and even picked out a new suit for you."

"She's just too much," I confessed.

"How so?" Tara asked.

"I know it is a crime to say this, and some would say that I'm ungrateful, but she was so sex crazed that I couldn't keep up with her," I explained.

"I can't believe you're admitting this. Come on, you are in your thirties. That is hardly old. How old is she?" asked Tara.

"She's twenty-something."

"Ha ha. Look out! And they say that women reach their sexual peak at forty. Let me get you a drink," Tara offered.

"Sure, I'll have a gin and tonic." Tara waved down the bartender as I continued, "Night and day, all the time she wanted it."

"You must feel so used," Tara said with mock sympathy.

"Not used, but tired," I said.

The bartender placed my G and T and a vodka tonic for Tara on the bar in front of each of us.

"Well, it's not just that, the strong libido was welcome most of the time but," I paused, "she's a biter."

"Hmmm, well, that's certainly not the kinkiest thing I've heard," said Tara.

I finished sipping my drink and put it back down on the bar, "The first time it happened, I thought she was just excited, but then she kept doing it and then she asked me to bite her back!"

"Really?" Tara exclaimed. "How hard did she bite? Was there any blood involved?"

"Yes, it's like she literally wanted to take a bite out of me. It kind of gives a new meaning to the phrase 'You want a piece of me?' " I joked.

"Well, I guess she really thought you were yuuuuummmy," Tara teased.

"This is no laughing matter. I have some serious welts and scars now."

"You don't think that you could just humor her every now and then? It doesn't seem too hard. And now you know precisely what she gets off on. Maybe you could 'convince' her to return the favor and entertain some of your fantasies," Tara suggested.

"Well it's about more than just humoring her. When we first started dating, she asked me to take a blood test to be tested for STDs. I had no problem with that. I thought she was just being cautious, but it turns out there was a specific reason she asked me to do that."

"Oh…" Tara said, her voice trailing off.

I continued, "Well, after the test results came back and I told her, she said that she was glad to know that she could be totally uninhibited with me."

"That doesn't sound so bad," said Tara.

"That's what I thought, too. At first everything was great. The girl liked it rough, and then one day she was so excited that in the midst of it, she bit me. When it happened, it really seemed to drive her wild. She asked me to pull on her nipple piercings and to bite her. I did bite her nipples pretty raw a few times because she told me to keep going and not to stop. Then, there were other times when she would bite me so hard that I bled. Another time she started licking this scrape that I had gotten after playing soccer. She said she wanted to soothe the wound. She seemed obsessed by it. She would say things like how she wanted to share everything with me blood-to-blood and how she felt so close to me. And, she felt safe with me now that we'd both been tested."

"She sounds like a vampire!" Tara said.

"That reminds me of this one time we were just bumming around and watching *The Bachelor*. She loved that show. Well, one of the girls in the house had these fang-like teeth. I mean it was noticeable. When the bachelor noticed it, he kind of played it off saying that he could see she had some vampire fang thing going on, and he thought it was hot. Gemma thought it was hilarious and she asked me if I thought she'd look hot if she got some work like that done to her teeth."

"Oh, I think I know the episode you're talking about. Yeah, we never got to find out if her teeth were real or cosmetically done," Tara added.

"That reminds me, one day, after I came home from a long day of work, and she answered the door in a skimpy red negligee," I said reimagining the scenario. "I soon discovered that there was nothing underneath. She was so hot. But when I leaned in to kiss her, she smiled and I saw that she was wearing some fake fangs!"

Tara gasped, "Really?!"

"Yes. Getting back to the story... I told her to take them off—the fangs I mean, well the rest of what she was wearing did not stay on for long either. As things continued, I tried to stop her from biting me all the time. I even tried not to be as rough with her during sex. But she would just sulk about it and say that the sex was not as hot as before. I told her that I wasn't really enjoying all her biting."

"So, in the midst of all this I take it that you had given her the keys to your apartment?" asked Tara.

"Indeed. One day I came home and half of my clothes had disappeared because she had donated them to Goodwill and reorganized my closet. So, I asked her for my keys back."

"Well aside from all of the biting and rough sex, it sounds like she really invaded your space," said Tara.

"More like she took over my space."

"I'm sorry to hear you had to go through all that." Tara smiled and looked at me and said, "There is seriously never a dull moment with you around."

Unbuttoned

(FRANK)

I was relaxing and sipping my usual glass of Chardonnay at the NoMad hotel, which has a nice, little upscale bar. As I reached into my pocket for my cell phone, I accidentally bumped the woman sitting next to me with my elbow. "Excuse me," I said as I took a second look at her. She was slender with refined features and had a very rigid and formal look to her as she was wearing a high-necked blouse buttoned all the way up to her chin under a conservative business suit. Something about her appealed to me even though she looked like she needed a few drinks to loosen up. "So, you waiting for someone?" I asked.

"No, I just needed a drink after a hard day at work."

"Me too. Can I get you another?"

"Sure."

The first drink led to a second, and then a third when we decided to move to one of the tables to have dinner together. This led to a fourth glass. By then, I learned that she was named Alexis and was originally from Newport, Rhode Island. By the fourth drink, she was fairly drunk and had unbuttoned two of the buttons on her blouse. I discovered that she lived close by in the Flatiron District and offered to walk her home.

She replied, "Okay, but no funny business. You are just walking me home."

When we entered her lobby, I realized that I needed to pee and asked if I could use her bathroom. She replied, "Okay, but no funny business."

We walked past the doorman and into her elevator. At her floor, we got out and she opened the door to her apartment. I followed her in and two things were obvious from the get go. First, this apartment was the darkest apartment I had ever seen and second there was a really bad smell to the place. In the darkness she pointed to a light four feet away and I walked toward it to find the bathroom. I closed the door and peed.

When I finished and opened the door, I was surprised to find Alexis completely nude in the silhouette of the bathroom light. "I thought you said no funny business?" I asked.

"This isn't funny. I very seriously want you to have sex with me." She led me in the dark to her bed and there the formerly buttoned-up woman was all over me. First, she unzipped me and put her mouth to work on my dick and moved into the woman-on-top position. I stopped her to put on a condom. As she slid up and down, she yelled in my ear, "Do me harder! Do me harder!"

We came at the same time and she collapsed on top of me. As soon as we were done, I knew that I had to get out of there pronto. So, I politely told Alexis that I had an early meeting the following morning and couldn't stay the night. It's not that I never ever wanted to see Alexis again, but I lied due to the terrible smell that had accosted my nose the entire time we were having sex.

As I exited her apartment, I looked down at my navy blue suit and saw that it was entirely covered in cat hair. I also noticed bags of used kitty litter near her front entrance. The mystery of the bad smell was solved! Alexis was a cat lady. Judging from the hairs on my suit, all those bags of kitty litter, and the smell in her apartment, she probably didn't just have one cat. She either had about ten cats in there or one huge mountain lion.

Postscript: About three weeks later, I was walking by a newsstand when I saw this headline: "Bengal Tiger Found in Woman's Flatiron Apartment". I had to pick up the paper, of course! As I read further for details, the news report confirmed that it was Alexis. Initially, she had brought the tiger over as a cub from Bangladesh, but now it had grown and was literally causing a stink for the neighbors. Unfortunately, for Alexis, one of them had reported her. I'm just glad the tiger was asleep when I was doing Alexis.

Letting Go
(TARA and ROXANNE)

Tara had not seen Willem for a few weeks. In the past when this had happened, it had been extremely frustrating for her because he'd suddenly become inaccessible and unavailable. But this time, it suited her just fine because she felt like she needed some distance after what Luana had told her at brunch. She really wanted to get to the bottom of it all.

Tara's Story:
The holidays were approaching, and I didn't want to go through Christmas and New Year's feeling confused and conflicted about Willem and my relationship with him. My phone rang, interrupting my thoughts. It was Roxanne.

"Hi, Tara. How have you been? I wanted to call because I know that you have been going through some stuff with Willem."

"Thanks Roxanne, you always seem to know when to call."

"Are you really okay with knowing what Luana told you? And are you really sure that all of this is in his past?"

"Yeah, I'm really confused because Willem said that this was in his past but then Luana told me that he still does this. She knows some of his clients. I don't think Luana would make something like this up."

"Well, there's only one way to be one hundred percent sure," Roxanne said mischievously.

"Just what are you suggesting?"

"I can try to find out how he conducts his massage sessions and if he is really giving magic orgasms."

I laughed. Roxanne always knew how to lighten the mood. "Magic orgasms? You are too funny! Okay, so, what's the plan?"

"He's never met me and he doesn't know that you and I know each other, so it's perfect."

"Yes, and I just want to know the truth and what I'm dealing with."

So, Roxanne made an appointment with Willem for a massage the following week.

Roxanne's Story:

Since Willem would be making a house call, I rearranged some of the furniture in my living room so that he could fit his foldable massage table there. I thought it would be best to keep things out of my bedroom. When the day arrived my doorman buzzed saying that Willem had arrived, and there he was at my door.

"Hi Roxanne? Hey, I recognize you from TV. You look just like you do on TV."

"Yes, and you must be Willem," I said holding out my hand for him to shake. I was dressed in a big, fluffy, terry cloth robe. I motioned him to enter my apartment. As I held the door open, Willem walked in with his massage table and equipment.

"You can just set up here in the living room," I told Willem.

"If you'd like to be more comfortable, this will probably fit in your bedroom," Willem suggested.

"Well, there's more space in this room than the bedroom."

"Okay, if that's your preference," Willem said as he started unfolding his massage table. Then he took out some candles and sticks of incense from his bag. "I hope you won't mind me lighting a few candles and incense."

"Sure, I see that you are setting the mood," I remarked.

"Speaking of which, I brought this iPod with some music to set the mood as you put it. Can I plug it in somewhere?"

"You can plug it into the iPod dock over there," I said motioning toward a bookshelf.

"Great," said Willem as he walked over to plug in and cue up the music on his iPod. "How about we dim the lights?"

"Sure," I watched Willem as he dimmed the lights. With broad shoulders and a lean physique, I could see that he was Tara's type. "I'm so glad that you are here now. I really need to de-stress and release a lot of deep tension," I said as I walked to the massage table that Willem had covered with a big plush towel.

"That's what I'm here for," said Willem.

"So, you'll give me a little extra special treatment and make sure you find my tight spots?" I said realizing this might bait him.

"Of course."

I excused myself, went to the bathroom, removed my robe, and covered up with a towel. When I returned, I lay face down on the massage table and moved the towel down to expose my back and cover my lower half. Relaxing meditative music played in the background and the scent of incense filled the room. Willem began applying some massage oil and lightly running his fingers with a featherlike touch up and down the sides of my body. Then he started doing this up and down my back in a way that actually turned me on although he had not touched me anywhere inappropriate. Willem certainly did have an incredible touch. I waited to see if he would start to actually massage my head, neck or back and rub out my tight spots, but he didn't. It was not quite like any massage I've ever experienced before. I thought about my ex, Cole, who would explore every inch of my body, figuring out my erogenous zones. He was a master at foreplay and knew how to work me up into such a frenzy that I'd have to have him. Before him I didn't know it was possible to have multiple orgasms. I hadn't experienced anyone with a touch like that since, that is, until now.

"Turn over," I heard Willem say.

It took a moment for me to register what he had said and that it was Willem who had said it. I slowly turned over onto my back with my eyes half closed. I felt him run his fingers along my arms and the sides of my body. Next, he started massaging my legs and inner thighs. Then, I felt his fingers reaching underneath the towel, in between my legs and I felt a yearning for his touch there, but then he started massaging my neck, shoulders, arms, and breasts. I started to lose myself in his touch as his hands moved down my torso along the sides of my body and down to my hips inching closer and closer and then they were reaching under my panties. Oh how I've missed your touch, your delicious mouth and warm kisses. I started feeling light-headed. Then as he started removing my panties it snapped me back to reality. He was not Cole. I was here on a mission for Tara. I forced myself to open my eyes and I saw Willem leaning over me. I could see that the slit in the crotch of his loose-fitting cotton pants was slightly open revealing that he had gone commando and was now aroused.

"Oh!" I gasped at the sight. "Willem stop. I just got an eyeful of something I don't think I want to see and I don't feel comfortable about this."

"I was planning to give you more than just an eyeful, if you know what I mean," Willem said.

"What?! Wait! No! Stop, that would make it worse, not better!" I said as I sat up, adjusting my panties and pulling the towel over me to cover up. "We are done here," I said firmly as I wrapped the towel around me.

"Come on, you knew what you were going to be in for. I am here to really help you de-stress."

"Well, apparently not. I didn't know the entirety of it. That I'd be getting a little show or that you'd be participating," I said as I slid off the massage table. "Just pack it up. Don't worry, I'll still pay you, but we are done here. Let me get you your payment." I walked over and turned off Willem's iPod, blew out the candles that he'd placed nearby, and turned up the lights in the living room. Then, I walked into my bedroom and got my wallet to pay him. When I returned, Willem had started packing up his massage table and things. I paid him and he promptly left.

Tara's Story:

The next day Roxanne called to tell me what had happened. I was disturbed and disgusted, but glad that I had found out about everything. It made it easier for me to finally decide what to do about Willem. Knowing what I now knew, I could not even consider a future with him. He was not the one for me. I wanted someone with whom I could build a future and with whom I could grow old.

It was December and somehow for the past couple of years, I always seemed to end up being single on New Year's Eve. But I knew that I wanted to start the New Year off right and everything about Willem now seemed wrong. So, when he called the following week and asked me how I was going to be spending Christmas and New Year's, I told him that I wanted to end it. I was ready to let go. There was no point in continuing things. Afterward, I felt relieved. It was like an early Christmas present, I thought. Well, maybe it was more like a secret Santa gift because it was one that I couldn't tell anyone about. Or, perhaps it was more of a Hanukkah gift, since Roxanne was Jewish.

I decided to thank Roxanne. So, I invited her to brunch that weekend.

"I've been invited to my friend Ryan Shemen's New Year's Eve party. His company Success with Teamwork organizes events year round and his New Year's Eve party is going to be at a sprawling loft space in Chelsea. You should come. It's guaranteed to be a good time," Roxanne said as she pierced her fork into a leaf of her mesclun salad.

"Thanks, Roxanne, I appreciate what you're doing, trying to lift my spirits and help me get my mind off of things."

"Ryan really does know how to throw a great party. He hires a DJ, has it catered, and there's lots of champagne flowing all night. His parties have infamously led to some love connections and even cemented friendships among a few 'bucket buddies.' Now, that's true friendship, someone who gets a bucket for you and holds your hair back when you aren't able to make it in time to worship the 'porcelain god,' " Roxanne said winking.

I took a sip of my latte, "Sounds like it could be a pretty crazy party."

"It's a good mix of people. There are always some of the same old familiar faces around, but then there are usually new faces, too. It's like we are all one big family of Ryan's friends and friends of friends," Roxanne said reassuringly.

"Roxanne, you're always so good at talking me into these things. Okay, I'll go, but on one condition: if you'll accept this," I said as I took out an envelope and handed it to her.

"What is this?" Roxanne asked excitedly as she opened it.

"It's a gift certificate for a full day of relaxing beauty treatments at the Plaza Hotel spa," I said. "After what happened with Willem, I thought that the least I could do would be to make sure that you actually got a real, full body massage," I said. "I thought that we could make a day of it and go together, sometime in the New Year."

"That's a great idea! We should go on New Year's day, to detox and recuperate after Ryan's party," Roxanne suggested.

What a great way to ring in the New Year. Things were definitely already starting to look up, I thought.

There's Someone for Everyone

(FRANK and Nine)

To blow off some steam after a long, stressful week, I had gone to the gym to play some racquetball. My cell phone rang as I was getting dressed after taking a shower.

"Hi Nine, what's going on?" I asked.

"I was wondering if you could do me a favor. Montoya was supposed to help me with something this coming Friday night, but he is working on a big case and he had to unexpectedly fly to Chicago."

"Okay, what's the favor?"

"I was going to go a speed dating event, but you are only allowed to attend if you bring someone from the opposite sex. Can you go with me?" Nine asked.

"Speed dating? Geez, I don't know."

"It would mean a lot to me, Frank, if you would go with me."

"Well, it wasn't that long ago that I bid on Tara at a date auction. Am I going to have to fend off unwanted suitors for you, too?"

"No, it's not like that. You'll have a chance to meet someone, too. It's all been taken care of. Montoya and I have registered for the event, so you can just take his place. Hey, I'll also treat you to a few drinks afterwards."

"Okay, I will give it a whirl," I replied.

"Great!"

Two days later on a Friday night, Nine and I found ourselves at an Upper West Side bar where the tables had been lined up in one long row. The men sat on one side of the tables and women on the other. Each couple had five minutes to get to know each other. After everyone had a chance to meet, we were asked to list the five people who we liked the most. Then, the host compared everyone's top five choices to see if there were any matches.

I had already talked to four women when I ended up sitting across from a pretty woman in her twenties who I instantly recognized.

"Hi, my name is Frank and I know that your name is Yvonne Channing."

"My name tag only has my first name on it. How did you know my last name?"

"A few months ago, you were in a date auction for the American Cancer Society, right?"

"Wow. Your memory is impressive. What else do you remember about me?" Yvonne asked.

"You are a Gemini, who loves to play tennis and to travel. You want a guy who is adventurous and you just learned how to cook," I responded.

"That is so amazing! How in the world did you remember all of that?"

"I never forget a pretty face or her personal information."

"Well, if I made such a big impression on you, why didn't you bid on me?"

"I was there for my friend, Tara. She asked me to bid on her, but she was the last one to be bid on and you had left by then. She was worried that no one would bid on her or that some pervert would bid on her. So, since I could only bid on one person, I couldn't bid on you."

"You must be a really good friend to do that for her."

"I'll say. I was planning on talking to you at the end of the event, but you left early after the guy bid on you. Was it at least a good date for you?" I asked.

"Actually, it wasn't a good date at all. He was something of a jerk."

"It isn't often you get a second chance in life," I said warmly. "Let's not tempt fate a second time. Forget these cards. You're the only one here I am interested in. Hang around 'til the end of this event and let me take you out to dinner."

"That sounds like a great idea," Yvonne said happily.

At the end of the event, Nine approached as I was talking with Yvonne, so I introduced her to Nine, "Yvonne, this is my friend Nine. I came here tonight as a favor to her."

Yvonne shook hands with Nine, and then she turned and said to me, "Are you always such a hero to all your women friends? Helping out damsels in distress?"

"Frank is a knight in shining armor." Nine put her hand on my shoulder and said to me, "You're a true gentleman."

"So, are you vouching for him?" Yvonne asked Nine.

"Yes I am," Nine said smiling.

"Frank has asked me to have dinner with him."

"Frank, I still owe you a drink but let's do it some other time so you can have dinner with Yvonne."

I realized that Nine was bowing out gracefully so that I could spend some more time with Yvonne. "Thanks, Nine, I'm glad you dragged me out to this event," I said.

"Have fun," Nine responded as she put on her jacket and got ready to leave.

I took Yvonne to a new trendy restaurant that was close by. At the end of the date, I gave her a single sensual kiss on the lips. The second date we went to a jazz club and again I gave her just one single kiss at the end of the night. On the third date, I took her to dinner at a cozy, candlelit Mediterranean restaurant. It was the sort of place that really enhanced the mood for romance.

After we ate, I leaned in to whisper in Yvonne's ear. "I usually make a move before the third date, but you seem very shy so I didn't want to rush into anything," I said putting my hand on her hand.

"I know. You are a special man."

"Is it okay if I make a move now?"

Yvonne didn't say anything. She just nodded and smiled. I leaned in and started kissing her gently, then moved to her neck and back to her lips. We made out for about half an hour.

Then, Yvonne looked at me with a serious look on her face. "Frank, I hope you go very slow with me. I haven't been with many men. I can't take you home tonight."

"That's okay," I responded.

We had been dating for about a month, when I started to reach under her dress as we were sitting in a cab one night, but Yvonne stopped me. Seeing the frustration on my face, she leaned in and whispered in my ear, "Frank, let's go to your apartment."

"I thought you'd never ask."

"You will be gentle with me won't you?" Yvonne asked sheepishly.

"Without a doubt," I said reassuring her.

Once we were in my apartment, we started making out on the sofa and then I led her into my bedroom. On the bed, I started removing her clothes as we continued to make out. When she was totally nude, I removed my clothing and went to a dresser drawer to take out a condom.

"Frank, I have something important to tell you."

"You have a special position you like?" I wisecracked.

"I have no positions at all. I have no experience at all. I am a virgin," Yvonne said with a look of seriousness to her face.

"You're serious? A virgin? How? You've never been with a man?"

"Never. I go to Catholic mass every Sunday. I am a devout Catholic. I've waited a long time. But I think I am ready now, with you. I just thought you would want to know that before we did it."

I sat on the bed and put the condom to the side.

"What is it Frank? Did I do something wrong?" Yvonne asked nervously.

I turned to her and kissed her on the forehead. "No, you've done nothing wrong. I grew up Catholic but I am now an agnostic. I'm not devout at all. I haven't dated anyone devout for a long, long time. And a virgin! It's just that I take that very seriously. To be someone's first is a big deal. Why me as your first?"

Yvonne covered herself with the bedcovers. "You are such a gentleman. I want a really good guy to be my first."

"I'm not that good. As a matter of fact, some would call me a player. The longest relationship I've had in the last four years has only been three months. You should be with a guy who can commit to being in a long-term relationship with you and I don't think that guy is me," I said in a sad tone. "There is someone out there for you."

Yvonne looked at me with tears in her eyes, "But I want you to be my first."

"I can't. I'm sorry. I was burned four years ago by a real bitch of a woman. I don't think I have recovered yet from that. I don't want to hurt you."

I went to the bathroom to grab some tissues and handed them to Yvonne to wipe her eyes.

Yvonne got dressed as I put on a robe. I walked her to my door and gave her cab money.

Later on, I text messaged Yvonne to make sure she had gotten home all right.

As I tossed and turned that night, I thought about my conversation with Yvonne. I heard my own words to her; 'There is someone out there for you.' And then I thought about one of my employees, Luke, who I knew was a devout Catholic.

The next day I called Yvonne, "How are you feeling?" I asked.

"Embarrassed," Yvonne responded.

"There's nothing to be embarrassed about," I reassured her. "Listen, there is a guy who works for me who I know is also a devout Catholic. He is really a good guy. From what I know of him, he is not the type to date around a lot. But of the few past girlfriends he's had, I believe that they have all been Catholic. That's important to him. I think he would be a better match for you. Would you mind if I gave him your phone number? Do you trust me to do this?"

"Yes, I do. Okay I'll give it a try. Thanks so much for doing this for me," Yvonne responded.

"And please, don't view last night as a rejection. Look at it as a blessing in disguise. Luke is the name of the man I want to introduce you to. I will tell him about you and that I think you would be perfect for him. Knowing him the way I do, I know for a fact that Luke will call you this weekend. I promise."

"You won't tell him about last night?"

"Of course not."

"Okay, you can give him my number," Yvonne said.

I learned that the next day Luke called Yvonne and they immediately hit it off on the phone.

Even though it had been over a month since the speed dating event, Nine had been insisting that she take me out for a drink as she'd promised. Besides, she wanted an update on what had happened with Yvonne and me. When Nine and I finally met up, I told her what had happened with Yvonne.

"Can you believe that? A virgin in Manhattan? She has to be one in a million." I said.

Nine gave me a serious look.

"What? Did I say something wrong?"

"No, you didn't. It's just that there are probably many more virgins in New York than you think. I go to a church with over a thousand people. There are also many other churches similar to mine. Then, there are all the Catholic churches. I am assuming there are probably thousands of virgins in New York City. Virgins are not as rare as you think," Nine asserted.

"Well, since I don't date devout Christians or Catholics, I don't run into them that often," I said.

"But I have to say Frank, that what you did was fantastic," Nine said with tears in her eyes.

"Hey. Hey. Why the tears?" I asked putting my arms around Nine, giving her a hug.

"It just makes me very glad and very proud to say that you are my friend. Most guys wouldn't have done what you did. You really are a knight in shining armor," Nine said proudly.

Postscript: I stayed in touch with Yvonne. Six months later, Yvonne and Luke were married. They had both agreed to wait until their wedding night as husband and wife to be together for their first time.

The Scarlet V

(NINE)

Frank couldn't tell, and I know that he is a very insightful guy. But he couldn't tell with Yvonne or with me. I used to think that people could tell by just looking at me. They could tell that I was a virgin, like I was wearing a scarlet letter of some type. I imagined myself being like the lepers in The New Testament screaming in the streets, "Unclean! Unclean!" announcing my presence and warning others of my condition.

However, in my case, I would be screaming, "Clean! Clean! Prude! Prude!" forewarning others. I didn't exactly set out to become a twenty-six-year-old virgin, it just happened. I have always been a Good girl with a capital "G." The Bible is very clear about not having sex until marriage and I wasn't going to give it up to just anyone. I would have to be married to a man before having sex with him.

Being an Air Force brat, I didn't always have a lot of stability, but the strong Christian values that my parents instilled in me have kept me grounded. As a child, we moved to a series of places, before ending up at Scott Air Force Base in Illinois. When I graduated from high school, I wanted to stay close to my parents. Being an only child and knowing that they would miss me, I went to Wheaton College, a Christian college in suburban Chicago. I would go home every weekend.

After college, I went to the University of Chicago Law School, also staying close to home and visiting my parents on the weekends.

While in my first year at law school, my father was promoted to the rank of Brigadier General and he and my mother moved to the Washington, D.C. area so that he could work at the Pentagon. I guess they both realized that I was finally mature enough to leave the nest and be on my own.

For my second summer in law school, I decided to go to the East Coast to be a Summer Associate at a corporate law firm in Manhattan, where Montoya was already a Partner. He was the one who did my on-campus interview, and later became a mentor to me. After I graduated, the firm gave me an amazing offer, so I decided to move to the Big Apple to make my mark in corporate law. I was to report to someone else but Montoya continued to be my unofficial mentor.

My parents were not worried about me since my older cousin Trent, who was already living in Manhattan, promised to look after me. The first week I arrived in New York, Trent introduced me to several of his friends. One of them was Belinda. She was ten years older than me and she owned a well-known art gallery on Prince Street. Tall with big boobs, she would always dress fashionably, and in a sexy way, showing a lot of cleavage.

"I'm glad that my cousin Trent arranged for us to meet," I told her when we first met.

"Nine, I think I need to keep you under my wing. You definitely need some looking after," Belinda said protectively.

Belinda would bring me to all the big parties and I would hobnob with celebrities at all the clubs. I usually limited myself to two glasses of wine a night since I didn't want to get too tipsy. At these parties, I met a dashing up-and-coming male model, a rap star, several hedge fund head honchos, and more actors and actresses than I could count. But every time I thought I made a connection with one of these celebrities, Belinda would butt in and make a point of saying that I was "her innocent little sister." Some people deciphered the code and realized that meant I was a virgin, or inexperienced at the very least. It used to bother me as if there was something wrong with me.

Then, I found The Journey Church and attended one of their growth groups and really liked it. Half a year later, I was co-leading a Journey growth group. Every growth group met for thirteen weeks to discuss a Christian book and at the end of each meeting, the group members shared prayer requests. Part care circle and part book club, it helped me to make some good Christian friends in New York.

At The Journey Church, it was not only okay to be a virgin; it was respected and admired. Because of the acceptance I got at The Journey, I no longer felt insecure about being a virgin, so I finally broke ties with Belinda. She was angry and told me that I needed to grow up. But the thing was, I didn't need to grow up. I had outgrown her, and I didn't need to be under anyone's wing anymore.

The New Hunter-Gatherers

(NINE, Luana, Katia, Tara, Roxanne)

The five of us had gathered for a girl's night out on a chilly Valentine's Day. It was the perfect weather for hot pot at Sik Gaek, a Korean restaurant in Woodside, Queens. I had suggested the restaurant based on the recommendation of my friend Cindy Zhou, who ran a foodie blog called *Chubby Chinese Girl*. Cindy had said that dining at Sik Gaek would be a truly unforgettable experience. And we were about to learn why.

The drama that had played out between Luana and Gianni right before Tara and me at Juan's party was now a distant memory. Since then, Luana had broken up with Gianni and had become a part of our circle. Luana had invited Katia, and Tara had invited Roxanne.

We ordered a bottle of rice wine while we waited for the seafood hot pot to arrive. The center of the table had a built-in gas range. The hot pot, basically a pot of broth, was placed right on the gas range. Next came a large bowl of seafood, which was to be placed into the hot pot once the broth had started boiling. In the bowl was a giant squid still slithering about; there was also a lobster, a crab, and several other things that were all moving in slow motion. The bowl seemed alive with creatures. It looked like a scene out of the movie, *Alien*, with Sigourney Weaver.

But here there was no big mama alien; these were just little baby aliens. The roles had reversed. Instead of aliens hunting down humans and taking over their bodies, we were the hunters and ready to stuff ourselves with these edible little aliens. Our server, who was wearing plastic gloves, took out a pair of little scissors and started cutting the tentacles off the squid. The squid watched in horror as its tentacles were severed one by one. When only the squid's head was left, the server cut that into three parts. The lobster was next, after witnessing all of this; it seemed to be trying to escape out of the bowl. Poor thing, it didn't make it. First to go were the claws, then the tail. Finally the little guy was cut in half—right down the center. Into the pot he went with the squid. Next was the crab. After five minutes, practically everything in the bowl had been transferred into the hot pot.

Some bits and pieces remained in the bowl. I couldn't stop staring as I noticed one of the squid's severed tentacles still clinging onto the bowl for dear life, and said, "I have never ever had food that fought back. I can see why some people become vegetarian."

Tara took photos of the bowl with her iPhone. Our server instructed everyone on how to use the dipping sauces and scooped the tentacles from the hot pot while they were still moving. Roxanne was already tipsy because instead of the rice wine, she has been downing soju. Her trademark mass of blonde curly hair contrasted with her flushed face. She fanned herself as the steam from the hot pot floated over the table. Her loose blouse almost fell off her left shoulder.

"It seems like people in New York are always looking around to upgrade, and men especially, always try to date out of their league," Roxanne complained.

"You mean like upgrading from coach to first class? What's wrong with that?" I interjected.

Roxanne continued, "Well, the other day I was at the Harvard Club's annual beer fest and this old, old guy comes up to me. He must have been at least eighty years old. He started talking to me and soon it was obvious that he was trying to pick me up."

Katia spoke up, "Can't blame a guy for trying. I love a dirty old man. They know how to treat a lady well. Big spenders."

"No, I'm angry," Roxanne responded. "How could he think that he had a chance with me? Eighty years old! It's insulting! He's looking at me like he's starving with desperation, like he's looking into a bakery window and I am the most decadent cake in the window."

"So, he finds you attractive? Isn't that a good thing?" asked Luana.

"No, you aren't getting it. It's all about leagues. Men and women are both guilty of it. Those who are eights want a nine and all nines want a ten. There are even some sixes or below who are trying to get nines and tens! I mean, be realistic. Don't set yourself up for disappointment or rejection," Roxanne continued with her rant.

"So, if you are an A cup, you secretly wish you were a B cup. And all the B cups want to be a C cup. Is that what you mean?" I asked.

"No, that's not what I'm talking about Nine," Roxanne responded.

"I think what Roxanne is talking about is level of attractiveness. It's like how some men and some women always go for the model types," Tara explained.

"Right! I told this guy... I am not your cupcake! I may be the most decadent cake you see in the window, but I am not for you!" Roxanne continued.

"And what you are saying is, how dare this guy think that he is even close to your league?" Tara asked.

"Exactly!" said Roxanne.

"The problem with men is they aren't satisfied with just one cupcake," Luana added.

"Are you saying that either everyone is trying to date out of his or her league or that no one is ever satisfied with who they're with? That's a pretty sad state of affairs. Remind me not to talk to any of you whenever I am depressed about my dating life," I said joking.

Katia interrupted, "I think that in New York, especially, there are so many options that men and women are always just looking to upgrade."

"And the grass is always greener on the other side. If people are married, then they wish they were single. And people who are single want to get married," Tara added.

"Listen ladies, I will give you the best advice you ever got," Katia said with an air of authority. "There is nothing wrong with dirty old men hitting on you. It's not about leagues; it's about money. But if you are going to go for an older guy, don't go for someone who is in his fifties or sixties or seventies. Go for someone old, I mean really old. They have to be in a wheelchair, with a walker, a cane, something that lets you know they are one step away from kicking the bucket. I mean someone in his eighties or nineties. If you go for someone under eighty, there might still be some gas left in the tank and they will still want some action every once in a while. You need a guy who might have a heart attack or a stroke just from seeing you get naked in front of him."

"Look, I don't want a guy for his wallet. I want a man with a hard dick and a strong sex drive. But too many guys are *um mala,*" Luana responded.

"What does that mean?" I asked.

"That's a Brazilian expression for a suitcase without a handle. I guess the closest analogy would be a drag—the guy is a drag—like a suitcase without a handle. *O cara e um coitado.* The guy is a loser. He doesn't get the job done, or know how to satisfy a woman. Those guys, they should just have a big letter 'L' tattooed onto their forehead as a warning to all women everywhere," Luana proclaimed.

Roxanne spoke up. "If anything gets tattooed on the guy's head, maybe it should be how good he is in bed."

Luana and Katia high-fived her.

I interjected, "I don't have a lot of experience with sex, but I do with kissing and making out. To me, a guy will never get far if he doesn't know how to kiss."

Tara added, "There is no way a guy can be good in bed if he doesn't know how to kiss."

Luana chimed in, "I'd agree with that."

"It is a damned shame when a good looking guy slobbers all over you or sticks his tongue down your throat," Roxanne added.

"So, would you agree that a good kisser makes up for average looks?" Tara asked.

"I really need them to be cute before I even kiss them," I responded.

"Its all about the money and their generosity. Not the size of their dick, but the size of their wallet," Katia said as she took a swig of the complementary cucumber juice that the server had brought to the table. "As for a man's kissing and other techniques, well, that can be taught."

"No, I have my own money. I want a man who knows how to use his equipment! I don't want some selfish, self-absorbed jerk, nor will I stand for someone clueless and inexperienced. He should know how to please a woman and want to please a woman in bed. There are just too many amateurs running around out there," Luana proclaimed.

"I want them to be madly in love with me. I will take love over kissing, having sex, or money," I told the group.

"The other day I was with this guy," Luana spoke up. "He was average in size, not huge or anything, but he was so passionate, it made the sex so hot."

"It's like they say, it's the motion of the ocean, not the size of the ship, but you do need a minimum-sized ship to even make a wave in the ocean," Tara said.

"I talk dirty and I scream in his ear... 'Give it to me! Give it to me!' " Katia chimed in. "Makes them hard and produces buckets. Everybody wants to be wanted."

"So, swallow or spit?" Roxanne wisecracked.

"I like taking a little in my mouth to show the guy that I accept him, but not swallowing massive loads," Luana responded. "I like pulling his legs apart and putting my head in between his legs and grabbing both of his hands as I give him the blow job of his life. That way, he is totally at my mercy and he can't use his hands to push and pull my head up and down."

"So many guys think your head is like a seesaw in the playground. Keep your hands to yourself and I will give you a blow job that you'll never forget," Katia declared.

"Wow, you ladies are so open!" I said amused by all the revelations and advice I'd heard.

"There is nothing to it. Just enjoy having it in your mouth. Act like it is the best tasting lollipop you've ever had. Lick it, suck it, and kiss it. Also, tickle and suck the guy's balls and he will be groaning in ecstasy," Katia instructed. "What's harder is teaching a guy how to give oral sex to you. God! Men and their fragile little egos! They don't like to be instructed. Make use of your tongue, be creative, get in there and enjoy it! Lap it up and drink it like it's an oasis in the middle of the desert! But if a guy doesn't want to go down on me, I will pull my panties up and be out of that bedroom faster than you can say 'lousy lay.' "

"That's right ladies, it's time for men to stop being cavemen when it comes to pleasuring a woman. Show 'em how it's done, tell them how it's done, and help them to improve on their technique. You'll have a better time. Think about it this way, even if you don't end up with him, the next woman will thank you for what he's learned," Roxanne added.

We ordered another round of drinks and I suggested a toast, "Here's to women and to us finding the men who deserve us!"

TO BE CONTINUED in Metropolicks Book 2...

ABOUT THE AUTHORS

Felicia Lin is a Taiwanese American writer who was born in Fairbanks, Alaska and raised in Ottawa, Ontario, Canada. She has a bachelor of science degree in Accounting from the University of Illinois at Champaign-Urbana and a master of arts degree in Applied Psychology from New York University. Currently, she resides in New York City. To learn more about her visit: www.felicialin.com.

Victor Scott Rodriguez is a native New Yorker, born in Brooklyn, and raised in Brooklyn, Queens and Manhattan. He has a bachelor's degree in Communications from Hunter College, a bachelor's degree in Religion from Rutgers University and a master of arts degree in Divinity from the University of Chicago Divinity School. Currently, he resides in New York City. To learn more about him visit: www.victorscottrodriguez.com.

Find Out What's Next for Metropolicks

VISIT www.Metropolicks.com

JOIN our mailing list to learn about events, news, and special offers.

WATCH us on 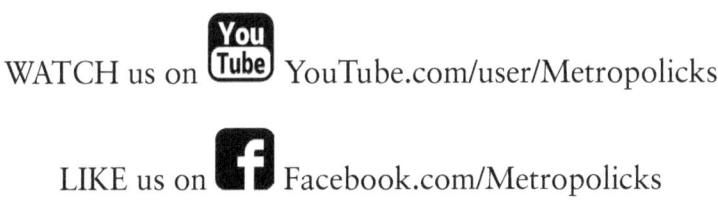 YouTube.com/user/Metropolicks

LIKE us on  Facebook.com/Metropolicks

FOLLOW us on  @Metropolicks

CONNECT with us on Linkedin.com/company/ Metropolicks

PIN us on Pinterest.com/Metropolicks

FOLLOW us on @Metropolicks

DISCLAIMER OF ENDORSEMENT

Reference contained in this novel to any specific commercial products(s), service(s) by trade name, trademark(s), manufacturer(s), organization(s), institutions(s), corporation(s), the appearance of external hyperlink(s), church(es), place(s) of worship or otherwise, does not necessarily constitute or imply its endorsement, recommendation, or favoring by any of the heretofore referenced or any governmental agencies. The views and opinions of the authors expressed herein do not necessarily state or reflect those of those commercial product(s), services(s) by trade name, trademark(s), manufacturer(s), organization(s), institution(s), corporation(s), the appearance of external hyperlink(s), church(es), place(s) of worship, governmental agencies or otherwise, and shall not be used for advertising or product endorsement purposes.

Neither of the authors has financial interest by the reference to any specific commercial product(s), services(s) by trade name, trademark(s), manufacturer(s), organization(s), institution(s), corporation(s), the appearance of external hyperlink(s), church(es), place(s) of workshop or otherwise nor has any specific commercial product(s), service(s) by trade name, trademark(s), manufacturer(s), organization(s), institution(s), corporation(s), the appearance of external hyperlinks(s), church(es), place(s) of worship or otherwise, paid any monies to the authors to be referred in the novel.